DECEMBER 2020 - ISSUE 171

FICTION

NON-FICTION

Neil Clarke: Publisher/Editor-in-Chief
Sean Wallace: Editor
Kate Baker: Non-Fiction Editor/Podcast Director

Clarkesworld Magazine (ISSN: 1937-7843) • Issue 171 • December 2020

www.clarkesworldmagazine.com

The Island of Misfit Toys

FIONA MOORE

Call him Santa, because why not. It's not the name he was born with. But it is the name he was called most often: by the kids who'd yell at him as he limped down the street with his sleeping bag open and wrapped round him for warmth, by the shopkeepers firmly pushing him out of their well-lit doorways, by the staff of the cheap restaurants he'd spend his carefully counted panhandling cash at.

It was the beard. The big off-white beard that spilled over his chest, easier to grow it than to spend time and money cutting and shaving. He'd also, despite his lifestyle, retained the belly he'd acquired through twenty years in a cubicle as a software developer for a company that made artificially intelligent Things. That was before the downward spiral that started with the redundancy notice and ended with him being tormented by children as he tried to grab a few minutes' sleep next to a dumpster.

But mostly it was the beard.

Something about his vague, lost, shambling demeanor made him a target. Despite his general air of Santa-ish-ness. Maybe *because* of his general air of Santa-ish-ness; it might have triggered memories of childhood frustrations, longed-for presents not delivered or the loss of innocence when you find out it's your Dad all along. Or else vague associations with capitalism, and all its hypocrisies: the genial bearded man whose generosity is a front for a hard sell.

On a certain freezing night, Santa, turned away from the Salvation Army hostel and having trouble finding the mosque where the imam would let you sleep on the office floor if you were out by the first call to prayer, was set upon unusually viciously by a group of teenagers drunk on supermarket-brand vodka and frustration. They took his money, they took the half sandwich he'd saved for later, they even took his sleeping bag, though it was no use to them and would only be thrown in the river later on. They kicked his soft belly over and over, and then, when he was no longer giving them any more entertainment than feeble cries, one of them was inspired to grab a piece of discarded lumber and hit him with a crack on the head.

There was a moment of awful silence as they realized that the game had gone much further than they'd planned. Then a general scattering of bodies, the sandwich dropped at the mouth of the alley. Not waiting to see how badly he was hurt, or even if he was still alive.

And all because he hadn't been able to get to The Island.

The Park, like most big city parks of the time it was established, had a small river and an ornamental lake, something for fashionable Victorians to stroll around pretending to enjoy nature. In the middle of the ornamental lake was The Island: a patch of rocky turf just large enough to support an ecosystem of trees, bushes, and birds. At one time you could hire a boat, enjoy a picnic. Or swim out there, though, in the absence of a beach, there was not much to do once you'd done that other than swim back again. Those days were gone, however; the city was concentrating its funds on the mainland. There were no more boats, and few people were enterprising, determined, and healthy enough to swim.

But Santa was enterprising and determined, and he'd been on the swim team back in the days before the belly. So when he could, he'd stash his things in the most leakproof plastic bag he had, and breaststroke out there.

He could spend days on The Island. Enough woodcraft came back to him to allow him to weave a little rain shelter from Scotch pine boughs, and he would spend hours enjoying the antics of the squirrels and birds, or peering back at the mainland, watching the people in The Park without them knowing they were being observed.

But when his resources got scarce, he had to come back to the shore. And in the winter, the cold was too severe for him to risk sleeping in the open. Hence why Santa was now lying in an alley, blood soaking his off-white beard.

Sometime later, Santa returned to consciousness.

He didn't know where he was, and his head hurt. He tried to focus, couldn't. Got to his feet, staggered out of the alley, trying to find an emergency room or a shelter or any safe place, slurringly trying to articulate what he needed. The people still about at that late hour avoided him, assuming him to be drunk or high or having a delusional episode. Finally, he found himself huddled up in a waste management site on the edge of town, the rotting garbage making the area slightly warmer and comparatively inviting.

By this point, the effects of the beating were starting to wear off, or at least settle down to a general background hum of pain, and so Santa decided to cut his losses and spend the rest of the night there, and see about the emergency room in the morning.

When he saw it, he thought at first that it was one of the aftereffects of the crack on the head.

A little, cheeky face, appearing over the side of a recycling bin. Pink fur ragged and matted, one eye scratched and dulled, but it still wrinkled its red nose and wiggled its ears in what was once a charming, friendly way (but now, since part of its muzzle had been broken, looked slightly creepy).

Santa still didn't quite realize what it was until he saw the other one. A bigdog, one of those Doberman-sized, six-legged things that crawl determinedly through rough terrain and up and down stairs, bearing deliveries or luggage or equipment. Its two back legs were nonfunctional, and it was dragging itself along the ground.

The law says artificially intelligent beings, if their bodies or minds are damaged, need to be returned to their manufacturer. The law also says that animals must not be abused, children must not be terrorized, and sad old men looking for shelter shouldn't be kicked and beaten just for a moment's entertainment.

It didn't surprise Santa that these intelligent Things were in the dump with him. Maybe the manufacturer had gone bust. Maybe for some people it was easier just to throw a sentient creature away than to take the trouble of sourcing an address or finding a deposit outlet. Maybe it was an act of hate, or abuse; Santa had seen enough that he could imagine someone breaking a child's beloved toy and making them watch while the little protesting thing was hauled away with the garbage. Or the child themselves, gaining some sadistic thrill from this act of torture.

Santa had no illusions about the innocence of children.

The pink creature spotted Santa, cocked its head, and asked him something distorted and incomprehensible.

He thought he might have programmed something like it a long time ago.

Taking an educated guess at what it wanted, he said, in a voice rough with limited use: "Yes. Let's play a game."

So they played a haphazard game of tic-tac-toe, using bottle tops from the garbage. The creature's memory of how to play was distorted, and Santa couldn't always understand what it was saying, but he did his best. Afterward it wanted to sing a song, which came out vaguely like "Jingle Bells," and Santa tried to join in as best he could. The bigdog sat down next to them and watched.

By the time Santa looked up, others had joined them.

A novelty mascot for a fast-food company, face fixed in a permanent smile that had once involved LEDs. A cleaning-bot, tottering on damaged legs, picking things up and then discarding them quietly, having no place to put them anymore. A security camera—unable to move, but Santa could see its lenses tracking back and forth from the top of a nearby heap. And lots of toys. Cute fuzzy animals, engaging dolls, build-your-own-AI projects, educational novelties for small children. Something that he suspected had once been a monitoring robot from a nursing home, one of those smiling roly-poly seal pups meant to monitor the life signs of frail elderly residents. Now with its head smashed in a way he didn't want to think about.

All of this was giving Santa an idea.

Once it had finished singing, he asked the fuzzy pink thing to come sit on his lap. Which it did, with scary enthusiasm. As it attempted to chirp and purr, Santa found the access hatch, opened it. Examined the damage.

Then, addressing his audience, he asked them to fan out, find anything that looked roughly like the pink thing, even if it wasn't moving.

Especially if it wasn't moving.

The Things dispersed; some clearly enjoying what they thought was a new game, others stolidly obeying a command. Some didn't understand, stayed where they were, so Santa began examining the damage on them, one by one.

Before long, he began to get a haul of broken pink things. Some later or earlier models, of varying degrees of compatibility. Some of the same model. A couple that turned out to still be sentient, just immobile.

Santa fixed up the original first. He couldn't get it back to factory perfection, of course, but with a little effort he got the components working well enough that it could walk and talk properly again. And, with his memory of how to reprogram by voice coming back, he began to expand the limits of its capability.

And set it to keep watch.

For the rest of that day, Santa fixed toys and bigdogs and security cameras and cleaners. It was slow work, but by the time the sun was starting to go down, he had a few little helpers.

The original pink thing sat on the top of the nearest heap, whistling like a prairie dog if it saw a human or a digger coming. He had another one up there before long. He slept in the junkyard again, this time guarded by friendly watchers.

The next day, he left the junkyard, a couple of cleaners in his pocket and an old surveillance camera in his bag.

Between them, they not only managed to shoplift enough food to keep him fed for a couple of days, but also some of the specialist electronic equipment he was going to need. Santa himself would stand in front of the store pretending to panhandle, until he felt the cleaners running up his frayed trouser legs, letting him know it was time to move on. He'd got them programmed to home in on him if he got forced out by the police or the shop owner, but they worked better than he expected, and they were always done before someone took exception to their presence.

This occupied Santa for a good few days, and also allowed him to improve his situation, as his little helpers also managed to acquire a rucksack and tent and new sleeping bag (the bigdogs and drones were particularly good at sidling innocently up to delivery warehouses and mega-kitchens as if expecting to take someone's order, and it turned out delivery employees weren't great at checking courier ID). Even got him some clean clothes, allowing him to take the deception further and pretend to be a regular shopper for a little while, at least if no one looked too closely.

And while he built up his little empire, Santa was developing a plan for its future.

They couldn't stay in the dump, that much was clear. He'd been lucky, and clever, and avoided detection, but eventually the odds wouldn't fall in his favor. Besides, it might be warm, but it smelled and was probably full of diseases. However, he couldn't go 'round the hostels anymore, not with a retinue of staggering bigdogs and skipping dolls and teddies.

The obvious answer occurred to him early on. But the problem was, how to make it work.

Could he really ferry all of them over to The Island without water damage? The flying ones would be fine, but the bigdogs ranged from the size of a poodle to the size of a Shetland pony, and most of the littler ones weren't built for rugged outdoor conditions. So he put the idea to one side, while he worked out all the possibilities.

And then, one night as he slept fitfully under a heap of warm mechanical bodies, he was awakened by many bright beams of light and angry voices.

"Told you there was some bum sleeping in here—right, you bastard, on your feet."

But he'd been expecting this for a while. He surged up, pocketing his smaller and less mobile friends, slinging up his rucksack, and, the bigdogs galloping in formation around him and the drones keeping up a buzz over his head, rushed at the lights and past them, toward the gate and out into the streets.

He ran until he was sure he wasn't being pursued, then slowed to a walk, choosing random directions and trying to keep his progress as quiet as possible despite the noise of the feet and servos and blades of his entourage. Fortunately the dump was on the edge of town, near warehouses and industrial parks, shuttered and dark in the cold.

Turning at random into an alley, Santa stopped.

And began to laugh.

The alley ended in a locked corral of floats, ready for the annual seasonal parade.

Right at the front, in red and gold, a huge, wheeled, sleigh.

It didn't take someone of Santa's newly honed skills long to hack the lock, then persuade the self-driving AI governing the sleigh to go along with his plan. Loading his flock into the vehicle, he sped off through the night, toward The Park.

In the morning, the sleigh was first reported as stolen by the local news stations, then, just as quickly, was found on the shore of the lake. The AI swore blind she'd been taken by masked joyriders and, eventually, with no more plausible story at hand, the city police accepted it; the parade staff were mostly concerned with restoring the sleigh to driveability in time for the event. It became one more silly-season item, and, by the time rumors began to circulate about the strange creatures park-goers occasionally glimpsed, or thought they glimpsed, on The Island, it had been forgotten.

Santa was doing all right for himself out there. His army of helpers foraged for him, guarded him, brought him news. He worked on them, made them tougher, amphibious, smarter. He spent the winter out there with them, warm in proper clothing and with a little solar heater for his camp.

Eventually the stories about The Island became common enough that the city felt they had to investigate. Drone flights only ever showed a single human-sized heat signature and blurry camera footage. And, come spring, when the police and parks maintenance teams mustered the resources to send boats over with the aim of arresting him, the people that made it out there only ever found a couple of broken bigdogs and toys, and decaying evidence of a hobo camp.

In the end, the official position was to call Santa and his helpers an urban legend, something to entertain colleagues with at a bar or make a stop on a dark-tourism walkabout.

So the situation continued for years and years, speculated on by locals, monitored at a low level by the authorities.

Until, one day, the human-sized heat signature disappeared.

A police boat dispatched to The Island was unable to find a corpse, and indeed none was ever found. It was assumed, given his presumed age and the stresses of homeless life, that he'd died, though of course there was also the never-disproved possibility that he'd moved on, to another city or town or out of homelessness altogether. Maybe he'd passed through a portal to Mars, or been bodily assumed into Heaven in a sleigh. The story-makers speculated endlessly, never reaching a conclusion, or, indeed, figuring out the truth.

Looking out to The Island today, if you're lucky, you can still see them.

A glimpse of movement in the trees, too precise and jointed to be a squirrel. A flicker of tiny plastic wings. A metal limb extending delicately out to touch the water's surface, then retreating before you can register what you've seen. Rarest of all, a small tribe of cute, big-eyed creatures, their fur long ago worn away, tumbling in a battered horde along the edge of The Island, stumpy limbs marching, singing a screechy tune that might once have been "Jingle Bells."

There's always those bold enough to swim or boat over, trying to grab one. But those who have, find their prey is too quick, or too clever, or (in the case of the teenager who followed one of the metal teddy bears into the copse only to get kicked mercilessly by a circle of bigdogs) too devious and vicious. So they're mostly left alone.

And every year, on the midnight that turns Christmas Eve into Christmas Day, The Island lights up in red and green bursts and pulses. The sound of discordant music, stamping feet dancing, and electronic howls. The icy water turns electric with flickering displays from LEDs, from emergency lights and warning horns, from features intended to amuse and educate a child, all repurposed into a symphony of joy. As, just for a moment, they remember who they were, and how they became what they are, and pay a mad, beautiful homage, wherever he is, to Santa Claus.

ABOUT THE AUTHOR

Fiona Moore is a London-based writer and academic whose first novel, *Driving Ambition,* is available from Bundoran Press. Her short fiction and poetry have appeared in *Asimov's, Interzone,* and *Mad Scientist Journal,* with reprints in *Forever Magazine* and *Best of British SF*; her story "Jolene" was shortlisted for the 2019 BSFA Award. She has co-written three stage and four audio plays and a number of guidebooks to cult TV series, as well as non-fiction articles for numerous print and online SF publications.

Things That Happen When You Date Your Ex's Accidentally Restored Backup from Before the Divorce

LISA NOHEALANI MORTON

It's unethical to pry the secrets you've always wanted to know out of your ex under the guise of "getting closure." The only reason you would need to know those things is so that you can turn around and use that knowledge on your partner, and that's a power you both agreed to forgo, when you got (back) together.

No matter how much you wish you knew when that business with Rudy *really* started, and whether it was before or after.

There are so many versions of a story that could have really happened. History is only writ in stone because it *did* happen that way, not because it *had to*. The backup insurance sells the idea of a rescue from unfortunate events—a resumption of life after a brief and medicalized caesura.

But sometimes mistakes are made. Sometimes a car crash and a transposed digit means the wrong body gets cloned, the wrong consciousness downloaded, and everyone's past gets just a little more blasted than they expected.

The lawsuits will go on for years, but as soon as your partner draws their first breath, they have constitutional rights, even under this court, and so they're processed and set free like any other clone, and of course they go straight to you.

Sometimes, you get a second chance.

Your relationship with the backup is a new beginning. The only way this thing has a shot at being viable is if you both treat the divorce like it never happened. Your partner and your ex stopped being the same person a long time ago, and if you hold them responsible for something another version of them did, you'll poison the whole thing from the start. *We have to build a new us, totally separate from the old*, you tell yourself.

You keep telling yourself that until you start to believe it a little. Enough, at least, to keep turning down your ex's invitations to lunch. Plenty of time to have that meal when your mind no longer boils with invasive questions, when you've regained some equilibrium and learned how to respect your partner's privacy.

Your partner's memories of that trip you took to Asheville together are clearer than your ex's are. Some of the things you've gotten up to in the bedroom recently remind you of that weekend more than anything between you and your ex had in years. Not the acts themselves, but the intoxicating excitement of discovering something new and wonderful with someone you've built so much of the old and familiar with. Seen through their eyes, heard in their gasps, everything becomes new to you again, too. You fall into exhausted, pleasure-drenched sleep, feeling their warm arms wrapped around you. "You're mine," they whisper in your ear, just before unconsciousness takes you. "Nothing could change that."

When the bombs hit downtown in the middle of the night, for the first time since you've been together, your partner still remembers the trick for helping you through a panic attack that your ex forgot or gave up on, over the years. They sit up in bed and pull your head into their lap, and rub your temples with their thumbs in tiny, gentle circles. You freeze and shake with every explosion, and you know their head must be haloed in the window by the overhead light in your bedroom, but your partner just keeps on soothing you, oblivious to the lateness of the hour or the danger.

They sit up with you for hours. You both have to get up early the next day, but they never say a word about it. They chug a second coffee and just keep moving.

When the nagging feeling that it's all going to happen again burns in the pit of your stomach, and you start tracking their movements and noticing statements that don't add up, you already know you're not going to leave without proof, so you don't spend too much time beating yourself up about it. You tell yourself it's not snooping if you're looking in their phone for the address you already know will be there.

It's closer to home than you expected, but it's there.

Most of the time, conversations with your partner are like things used to be, before it all fell apart. Their political beliefs haven't taken that weird turn into centrism; whatever happened to them that was so bad that they decided the costs of the war were too high, it happened after the backup was taken. They still support the resistance.

You're sympatico on the important stuff—*still*, you remind yourself, *not again, this is a different person*—and different enough on the details to keep things interesting. You recognize the person you fell in love with in the way they'll stay up half the night with you, dissecting a new concept or arguing over the best way to achieve your shared goals. You don't have to hide your mutual aid work, or the money and supplies you funnel to the resistance.

When you see them meeting up downtown with a leggy blond in a leather jacket and skinny jeans, you don't spend four agonizing months searching for some level of proof that will finally, against all your instincts, convince you that the thing that appears to be happening really is.

You do, without hesitation, the thing you should have done the first time. You call Tiana, and let her know your plans. You make sure you have a safe place to go, in case you need one.

Then you sit your partner down to talk about it. You don't hide what you know, or make them try to guess what it is you want to talk about.

"I know about the bombs," you say, with no other preamble. "And the boats."

You watch their face go from shock, to panic, to relief and blossoming joy as they realize you're not going to try to stop them. As they realize they don't have to hide it anymore.

They pull out their phone to signal their cell leader—the leggy blond, whose name turns out to be Rudy—and set you up for an introduction.

"Tonight?" they ask, muting the phone mid-conversation.

You start to nod, then shake your head. "Don't you have a date with Sydney?" Your relationship is no more closed than it was the first time, and they've been seeing someone new for a few months now. It's starting to look like a thing, although you haven't met their new paramour yet.

"Shit," they say, and turn back to the phone conversation for a minute. "Wednesday?" they say at last, and you nod, and they set it up.

The cell treats you as untrustworthy for a while—*"Not* un*trustworthy," your partner murmurs to you in the dark. "Of unknown trustworthiness."*—but their trust comes with time. You start with simple courier gigs, and move on to more important assignments as your position with the cell becomes more secure. There are only a few steps between the cell and Shayna, the resistance's general in the mid-Atlantic, so it's a heady time.

Sitting in the back of a faux-dive bar on H Street, getting the latest real news from a courier (they can't censor in-person conversations, at least not yet), you feel as though a broken bone has finally set. Its splintered edges mesh back together, letting the muscles around it relax, and bringing with it a lessening, though not a cessation, of pain. Your partner glances over at you, and you see a similar relaxation in their face. *Finally, all the way together.* For the first time, this time or any other.

They take your hand under the table, and turn back to the courier to ask a question.

Your first gig together is new and familiar at the same time. You're sneaker-netting a flash drive to a member of a cell in Hyattsville, using a visit to a jazz night at a local meadery as a cover. The mead is good, and the band turns out to be made up of members of Airmen of Note, so the jazz is, as advertised, hot. While you wait for the contact to show up, you and your partner play a board game on the patio.

You don't know what's on the drive and haven't tried to find out, and you've never done anything quite like this before, even though the feeling you get when you meet your partner's eyes is the same one you remember from running duet gigs with Bunny, the first time around, after your ex bowed out of the resistance. It's the same fear, the same excitement, the same bone-deep sense of righteousness. The same knowledge that the two of you are making a difference to the only thing in the world that really matters right now, no matter how many normal lives are being carried on around you.

It's an intoxicating feeling, even more than the mead, especially when it's shot through with all the threads of what you and your partner mean to each other.

While you're standing outside the Food Lion in Upper Marlboro at ten o'clock at night, waiting for the dreadlocked kid in the wife-beater that you're supposed to hand the surveillance drones off to and only have a vague description of, your partner catches your eye from where they're standing lookout and grins, with an edge to it that's just this side of maniacal. They purse their lips at you, making the silent sign that the two of you have used to indicate affection ever since you started dating the first time.

They're twenty feet away and washed-out under the parking lot lights, but you'd know that expression if it were sketched on a napkin, let alone on your partner's dimly lit face, so the feeling comes through. Warmth and love and belonging wash over you, until you have to shut your eyes for a second to regain your composure. You want to go to them and fold them in your arms, kiss them like tomorrow is not just uncertain but entirely ruled out, but you just purse your lips back at them and blink back tears.

Just then, your contact skates up on a board that lights up in a rainbow wave, flashing bright in the darkness, and you struggle, dazzled, to remember the pass-phrases that let you know that this courier is the real deal and not an imposter.

When your partner's lover is shot and killed by security forces during a resistance op, you get that burning feeling of history repeating itself.

The two of you can't go to the funeral—as far as you know, no nonresistance connection exists between either of you and their lover—but a relative livestreams it. You spend money the two of you don't have, in secret, for a pristine device and a really *good* VPN. You even cough up the premium for custom geolocation services, although it'll mean ramen packets for lunch for the next month. You select an IP that resolves to a neighborhood in Chennai that could plausibly contain other, acknowledgeable mourners, for added verisimilitude.

There's a little room at the back of your house that might have been used as a nursery, once upon a time. You set everything up there.

Your partner walks into the nursery, surveys the setup, then turns to you, tears already forming at the corners of their eyes. You walk into the room far enough to reach them, and enfold them in your arms while they cling to you. You squeeze them tightly—once, then twice—and press your lips to their suddenly sweaty temple.

Pulling back, you stare into their wide, tragedy-filled eyes. They take a shaky breath, and their eyes flick to the door. You take their meaning, and you're moving before they have to ask. Kissing their temple once more, you turn and go, closing the door and leaving them to their private grief.

As you walk down the hallway, a chip of ice freezes in your stomach and grows into a block as you contemplate what's coming.

In the days after that, you help them grieve. You hold them when they need to cry, you leave them alone when they start getting prickly, you sit up long into the night and let them monologue about their memories and all the myriad feelings of loss that come with losing a loved one until they pass out, exhausted, in your arms.

Through all of this, you're braced for the signs—the growing disaffection with the movement, the burnout—that presage the inevitable. The increasingly strident questions about how this could all possibly be worth it. The new friends from sober, moderate circles, who convince them that they can be a voice for peace and bring an end to the hostilities. The drawing away from you that will only accelerate as the gravity of your relative political positions continues to pull you apart.

You fill yourself with a constant refrain of love, ringing its changes through your mind like a bell, telling yourself that the past is not prologue even while you're sure that everything is on the verge of collapsing.

You hold this posture of tension for several uncomfortable months, but the disaffection you're expecting never comes. Your partner mourns, and bitterly so, but it never overshadows and drowns out their feelings for you, or causes them to repudiate their life's work. They monologue late into the night about what their lover meant to them, and you stay up and listen, but in the end, when they're wrung out, tearstained, and heaving breaths like they've run a marathon, they cling to you like you're the last thing in the world, and say, *I'm so glad you're here. Thank god you're here with me.*

They start to take riskier gigs, though. Things that don't just hurt the regime, but embarrass it. Ops that risk retaliation and response with overwhelming force. You hear the warning bells in your head as loudly as anyone, but this is new, not like last time, and you don't have hindsight to guide you away from the pitfalls. You try to convince them to play it safer, but all they have to do is gesture vaguely at the world and you find yourself out of arguments.

In the fall, St. Louis is liberated. Then Knoxville. The autonomous zones in Baltimore grow and merge. They take control of several transit hubs and an old sewing machine factory, and range outward from there to attack and embarrass the regime.

The Inner Harbor is home to a band of teenage resistance marauders who call themselves The Surfin' Terps. Members of that merry band mark themselves by the turtle-shell bike helmets they wear whenever they're on the water. On boats, jet skis, or hover skimmers that hang uncannily above the surface of the water, the Terps harry and mock regime boats that try to approach the port.

The military is still staying out of the whole thing, so the resistance doesn't have to worry too much about shooting tonnage above the size of a sport fishing boat or a catamaran, although the boats sometimes approach from Tidewater in large numbers.

The Terps rule the waves, bobbing and weaving, the skimmers dipping from side to side in a way that appears to defy gravity. With sonic weapons developed by UMCP's engineers, and tasers stolen from the unmarked federal police force occupying the city, they drive the regime's useful idiots back again and again, jeering at them loudly each time the boaters retreat from their latest attempt.

Flanking the conflict on both sides are streamers, darting in and out of the edges of the fight on their skimmers, protected by the unspoken but violently enforced ban on attacking journalists and other bystanders. Neither side feels like it has sufficient propaganda momentum to claim a moral victory without carefully controlled coverage, and the international press gets into the game as well, making it even more risky for the regime to crack down. Videos with titles like "dOn'T pOiNT tHaT tHinG aT mE bOi" and "Derpy Terpies get their comeuppance" proliferate online, night after night, in an endless dance for dominance over the public conversation.

Your last mission together starts off bad and gets worse. It was supposed to be a simple extraction. Someone was meant to be snatched by the cops at a demonstration in Dupont, and you were supposed to play the part of a protester spontaneously leaping to her aid, one of many, peeling her away from her attackers and helping her melt into the crowd.

You've been a character in this kind of flash mob before. Whoever is feeding you intelligence from MPD has to be way on the inside, so the resistance gets advance notice of a lot of moves like this.

It's important to protect everyone you can. That's the secret to sustaining the movement. "We all stand and fall together," as Shayna declares in her videos.

You take up station next to your partner, hands and fingers linked, just two more semi-anonymous bodies between the arrestee and the Feds, making yourselves into human shields against the violence you know could come.

Every time you've done this before, the cops have backed down. It's inherent to your strategy. You show up with overwhelming numbers for this very reason—they can't kill you all.

Except they can, over time. They can give you the death of a thousand plausibly deniable cuts. They can wear you out on the shoals of "restoring order" and "protecting property." Each bit of brutality not covered by the press provides cover for the next round of escalation.

The size of the massacre that the cops are unwilling to perpetrate grows in proportion to their fear of losing. They turn the temperature up, slowly, while the pressure rises, and every resistance victory makes the next gig more dangerous. A greater and greater force of numbers is needed, as time goes on, to show them that you're not to be trifled with or retaliated against without consequences.

This time, somehow, the resistance misjudges that count, badly.

This time, the cops aren't willing to take their obvious L and walk away. This time, they fight.

Cop streamers weave their way in and out of the fracas; the resistance hasn't anticipated this show of force, so they only have one streamer of their own, chugging down the street on an old and coughing Vespa.

A chorus of "Stop resisting!" floats up from the ranks of Feds in their unmarked uniforms. Batons rise up and whip down in an old familiar rhythm. The cops beat you back, but their cries grow louder and more theatrically frightened, despite their dominance over your forces. Hamming for the cameras to keep that sweet qualified immunity.

"Keep your hands away from my gun!" one of them shouts, the well-known prelude to a kill. You exchange looks with your partner, not even glancing to see if anyone is going for the aforementioned gun. They nod. You break together for the exits before this goes wronger than it already feels.

They get you while you're running for the alley. "Keep moving," your partner urges, but they're kettling from both ends of the block, and they were uncharacteristically smart enough to block off the side exits, so that conveniently jumpable and well-scouted wall you'd marked on Monday is no use to anyone.

They surround you on all sides before you realize what's happening. They recite the required warnings so fast you know they never intended to give you a chance to comply. "Put your hands down!" "Stop resisting," "Stop going for my gun!" they chant in unison, as your heart falls into your intestines.

Then they open fire.

You dive behind the concrete pillar of the façade of a Greek restaurant just in time to escape their bullets. Your partner is not so lucky.

The first slug hits them in the rib cage as they're sprinting for cover, the surveillance video will later show. They throw their arms out to both sides and start to flail in pain and panic as the bullet bites deep into their flesh, plunging at a downward angle through one lung and a kidney. The highly publicized autopsy will note that this wound alone might have been enough to kill them, although it's not the only one they'll take.

Cataloging the rest of the shots is not worth it. You do it nonetheless, every time, in their ever-changing particulars, staring empty-eyed at the screen as the events of the day play out, over and over.

Freed by that first shot, the cops open fire as one. The explosive roar of the rest of their bullets almost feels like an afterthought, compared to the soul-piercing, life-ending power of that first one. You can't help counting them, though—the second, and the third, and the forty-fifth. The sight of your partner jerking under the fusillade is an image you'll wake up from for the rest of your life.

Your partner is killed just a few minutes before the cavalry arrives. Shayna herself shows up to extract you from your botched extraction, but you're too blinded by grief and rage and a formless, unending terror to appreciate the acknowledgement of your partner's importance to the resistance, or in fact to be aware of almost anything that's going on around you.

You help Shayna's forces drive the Feds back, and the sense of unity you feel as you push them out of resistance territory pushes the shouldering darkness from your brain, for a while, anyway.

You don't allow anyone to accompany you, long after midnight, to retrieve your partner's body. You bring it back in to the makeshift resistance camp, in the Walmart parking lot, stumbling in a fireman's carry that lets their sludgy blood soak into your clothes and your skin.

You resist the people who try to take the body from you at first, until Shayna jumps in front of you. Talking soothingly, like she might to a cornered animal, she keeps your attention until exhaustion or capitulation forces you to your knees and makes you roll your partner's corpse out across the painted lines of the parking spaces.

Seeing them lying there like that, something catches in your chest and your breath judders to a stop. Minutes pass before you can drag in a real breath in order to let out the wail that feels like the only thing you know anymore.

You learn how to breathe again, in fits and starts.

You feel like the pain will never recede, but gradually, it does. One day you wake up and go nearly two hours after breakfast before your throat closes up and you can only suck in air in great gasps punctuated by long silences, and it's the marker of the beginning of a new world.

The war goes on, behind the scenes, but everyone understands that you need some time to lick your wounds. They give you space. Shayna sometimes looks like she'd like to offer you more, but in the end she keeps herself to herself.

After a month or so, you start running gigs again—just simple courier runs at first, but eventually bigger stuff. Charlotte converts to autonomy, then Somerville. It starts to be worth tracking resistance territory on a map.

Six months later, you have lunch with your ex. It's the first time you feel able to look at their face without crying.

You meet them at the diner you grew up in together. It's long since closed and burned down, but it's neutral ground for you both in a way that's hard to explain. Your ex takes your elbow, and together you walk down the road.

"Well, of course, I don't have your way with words," your ex says, and you shudder at a phrasing that never sounded so smarmy before. Suddenly, you're desperate to live in a world where everyone has at least a basic way with words, if not yours, and they speak their truths as best they can without an eye for concealment or power plays. Suddenly, you realize that for the past year that has stopped sounding like a luxury.

You ex's tone is a bit whiny, and why have you never noticed that before? How can they be nothing like your partner, when they *are* them? Disorientation sets in as you remember that once you considered your ex the original, and your partner the interloper.

A fresh wave of loss washes over you. The things that were lost, and the things that have gone before, and all the illusions that have fallen. "I'll have to see what the pod thinks of that," your ex says, and you realize, for the second time in your life, that the two of you will never be one soul again.

There are further exchanges, and further gigs, and ultimately the victory of the resistance against the regime, and this story continues on beautifully and gloriously long past this point, but this is the end of the story as far as you, your partner, and your ex are concerned.

That night, you stand before the mirror, thinking about your partner, and your ex. Thinking about how every story has versions, and the strange accident that allowed one of them to come to life, for a time. Thinking about how the alternate timeline can end up being one you endorse more strongly than the original.

You shiver in the October chill, not yet cold enough to turn the heat on. You hear your ex again, saying, "If you don't want to be alone—" an offer you kindly but firmly declined. You feel even more profoundly alone in the world than you did the first time.

Then you feel a strong pair of arms wrap around you, although no one is behind you in the mirror. A wave of warmth, love, and belonging washes over you, and you keep your knees from giving way by the sheer force of your terror that this visitation will disappear if you let yourself collapse. A warm, loving breath exhales into your ear, and you can somehow tell from the shape of the wind that it came from a pair of pursed lips. "You're strong," a soft voice sighs. "You're mine. Keep moving."

You give yourself up to the truth of the matter with a good will and a loving joy.

ABOUT THE AUTHOR

Lisa Nohealani Morton's work has appeared in *Lightspeed Magazine, Fireside Magazine,* and elsewhere. She is also one of the assistant editors of *Nightmare Magazine.* Writing as Ellen Cooper, she published *Congresswolf,* an interactive novel about werewolves, Congressional campaigns, and murder, through Choice of Games. Lisa lives in Washington, DC, with her partner and two cats. You can follow her on Twitter at @lnmorton.

The Last Days of Old Night

MICHAEL SWANWICK

Through chaos and old night, the three brothers journeyed. Sometimes they rode and sometimes they strode. When they rode, their steeds snorted cold steam from their nostrils and obsidian hooves struck sparks from the rock. When they strode, their feet sank in the earth to their ankles. The sky was lit only by witch fires. Sometimes there were moons or flotillas of comets. Not tonight. Like all things, the sky and road changed at whim. In all the world, only the brothers could dictate what those changes would be.

That was simply how things were.

Goat-Eater was a great-bellied giant of a man. "There is some new thing ahead," he rumbled. Before them, the black mountains sank down to an ebony sea where blind waves crashed upon a beach as black as snow. It took a sharp eye to tell one from another, but he had that eye. Also, he could smell salt in the air. "It is made of water and it extends even farther than I can see."

"It is not what we fear, however," said Bone-Grinder. "I would know." He was smaller than the others, but more muscular and ungainly. One eye was missing and the other puckered; he had the mouth of a malcontent.

The third brother, who was nameless, did not speak and never had. Only he knew whether this was by necessity or choice. But he made a gesture indicating weariness. They had traveled far and hard and needed to rest.

No cities were near. Sometimes cities spontaneously sprang up, filled with music and motion and so ablaze with light that they could be seen half a continent away. Tonight the mountains were bleak and cheerless. So the nameless one pointed at a low knoll, turning it into a timbered drinking hall that soared halfway to their knees. Smoke lofted from its fire hole.

Dissolving their mounts to night mist, the brothers put off their size. They did not knock—their kind never did—but threw open the doors and stamped within. A fire roared like a dragon at the back of the hall. Faces pale, warriors leaped to their feet, sending benches clattering. Their thane, mighty in war and worthy in peace, drew his sword and, kneeling, placed it on the floor before the brothers.

"Meat," said Goat-Eater, and an aurochs carcass was roasting on a spit over the fire.

"Drink," said Bone-Grinder, and a page who an instant before had been a warrior hurried to proffer a two-handled silver drinking cup that had formerly been his helmet, foaming over with ale.

The nameless one spun the thane's throne-chair about and sat before the fire, glowering and rubbing his hands together. His brothers squatted by his side, one crunching on a rack of beef ribs, the other swilling down beer.

"This is noble meat," Goat-Eater said. "Perhaps it was once a king."

"The drink is missing something, however," said Bone-Grinder and at that instant a cat streaked by his foot in fierce pursuit of a mouse. With a sweep of his gnarled hand, Bone-Grinder caught the mouse and held it up by its tail to his squinting gaze. It had eyes like beads of jet and whiskers like white scratches in the air, and it struggled most prettily to escape. "Serving wench," he said, and a young woman stood before him, clad in a simple brown dress, her eyes lowered. The giant examined her critically. "Fewer teats," he said.

The maiden felt her body alter so that she had only two breasts.

"You must have a name," Bone-Grinder said. "I will invent a language for the occasion and choose a word from it for you." For a long moment he was silent. Then: "Mischling," he said, "bring me a barrel of wine and someone to drown in it."

Mischling scuttled across the great hall to obey.

Which was how she came to be.

Fear was a mouse's natural state. So Mischling did not feel she had lost much in her transformation: her tail, her whiskers, and her sleek pelt, yes, those she missed. But one who was in constant danger of cats and boots and casually flung eating knives could scarcely be more imperiled by being enlarged to human stature. Like all mice, she had been born blind; vision had come as a tremendous surprise to her. This transformation was but one more phase in her life.

In the kitchen, she overtoppled a cask as tall as she was onto its side. Like the popcorn machine and the microwave, it had come into existence in tandem with the knowledge in her head of its location. Appearing from nowhere, Pétur seized her from behind and kissed her neck. Minutes before, Pétur had been a mouse as well and possibly her mate. But shortly after her transformation, a corresponding change had come upon him and with it memories of a past that had never been. They two now shared a history and hopes that someday they would be wed. Together, Pétur and Mischling rolled the cask into the great hall and, with mallets, popped off the top.

Then Pétur climbed in headfirst and drowned himself.

Both Mischling and Pétur naturally regretted the deed, but one did not go against the will of the brothers. It was simply what had to be.

After Bone-Grinder had drunk down the quaff and chewed the boy's corpse to nothing, he willed into being a throne-chair for himself and said to Mischling, "Stand before me."

She obeyed. Mischling had been a woman for mere moments and had no idea what was expected of her. She trembled like a mouse.

"Don't be afraid of me—or I'll crush you like a bug."

"No, sir."

"No monosyllabic answers either."

"Yes, sir."

Bone-Grinder growled, "You don't understand what I'm saying, do you?" Without waiting for a reply, he said, "From now on, understand everything you need to understand," and enlightenment flowed into Mischling. With it came horror, for she now understood that he had the impulsiveness of an infant and the restraint of an avalanche. As did his brothers. There could be no predicting what they might do. "Now," Bone-Grinder said, "Sing us a song."

There was a stringed instrument in Mischling's hands and she knew how to play it. Striking the appropriate stance she sang:

In the beginning was everything and nothing—
A singularity called the monoblock.
No dimensions, no difference, no measurement,
Yet it contained the end of all things . . .

"There is no amusement in this song," Goat-Eater grumbled. He grabbed a back leg of Bone-Grinder's chair and tumbled him into the fire.

Howling with wrath, doubling in size, clothes smoldering, Bone-Grinder rose up and, seizing his brother, tried to wrestle him into the flames. In doing so, he knocked Mischling over. By the time she rose from the flagstones, both were giants again and entangled in combat, cursing and hitting each other with their fists. Their brother roared with silent laughter.

As the giants fought, the thane and his men fled, fearful of being crushed. Mischling took advantage of the confusion to escape unnoticed—save for the silent one, who missed nothing but did not try to stop her—into the darkness outside.

Having nowhere else to go, Mischling crept into the barn and burrowed into the straw for warmth. Then she cried herself to sleep, wishing that Pétur were there to comfort her and knowing that although the brothers had the power to bring him back, never in a thousand years would they do so.

The eternal, unending night closed over her, and she slept.

Mischling awoke to the brothers hooting and bellowing. At their command the walls and roof of the barn flew away and earth and straw flowed upward to become their mounts. This, in turn, revealed Mischling's presence. Bone-Grinder seized her arm and yanked her upright. She grew almost as large as they. "We'll take this one with us. She can clean our boots."

The silent one nodded agreement. "She'll need a mount too," Goat-Eater said, and created a saddle beast, smaller in proportion to their mounts as she was to the brothers. With her new power of understanding, Mischling realized that this was done deliberately, so that she and her steed would have to struggle to keep up. For the brothers were, she now knew, as petty as they were powerful.

They rode away, leaving the drinking hall ablaze behind them.

It was a long trek to the sea. Mischling and her steed were both winded well before they reached it. All three brothers rode their mounts up to their necks in the surf. "Become solid," one commanded, but the surf remained as it was. "Let there be a bridge crossing you," said the second, but neither was that so. The silent one scooped up a handful of seawater to drink and then spat it out. They turned and rode back to the strand.

"Here is a great mystery," said Goat-Eater, "though not the one we seek. For thisimmense, roiling thing is continually changing yet refuses to obey us."

"There are no answers here," said Bone-Grinder. "Therefore let us a create a city where answers may be found—and let that city be called Kiv."

The silent one gestured and a city arose, filled with foundries and knackeries and boatyards. Light from its forges and torches created a semicircle along the seaside; myriad people and horses and wagons filled its streets, as industrious as bees in a hive. Seeing this, the brothers alit and put off their size. So too, perforce, did Mischling.

"Swim out into the water," said Bone-Grinder to the steeds, "until you drown."

Watching the beasts dwindle and disappear, Mischling felt a crushing sense of loss. Her steed was the only thing she had ever been responsible for, and she wished she could have somehow saved it, even as she understood why she could not.

The brothers disguised themselves as beggars in ragged clothes. "You will go before us," said Goat-Eater, "and you will ask questions, for it is beneath our dignity to do so."

"What am I trying to learn?" Mischling asked.

"Whatever you may," said Bone-Grinder. Which Mischling understood meant that they had had premonitions of some essential change forthcoming in the nature of the world and feared it might diminish their power.

With that, the three sturdy beggars and one slight maid entered Kiv.

For a former mouse, Kiv was almost as terrifying as it was entrancing. Its twisty streets and sudden broad squares were hung over with paper lanterns and strings of electric lights so that every breeze made the shadows dance. The air was clangorous with machinery. Smoke pinched the nose. Purposeful men and women hurried in every direction. Wagons brought charcoal to the forges and foundries and vans carried crates of tools, spikes, and square head nails to the boatyards and sawpits. Torchlit docks and piers jutted into the sea all along the waterfront. Beyond them, in the yards, boats were being built, tarred, and fitted. Lean men sweated over woks in the cookhouses, child messengers darted through the crowds, and sturdy women poured copper into baked clay molds in the manufactories.

A young man in a leather apron was taking a cigarette break outside a smithy. "Why is everyone building boats?" Mischling asked him.

"We hope to be on the other side of the sea before the Sun comes up and changes everything," he said.

"Sun?"

"The Sun is a thing not easy to explain. It is a great ball that rolls over the sky and then disappears in the west, only to be later reborn in the east. It is brighter than any lantern. Yet it is so far away that if you were to ride after it, however fleet your mount, you would never arrive on its shore. It casts a light over all the world. Yet when it goes down over the horizon, it takes that light with it and all is dark again. It has a surface temperature of roughly six thousand degrees Kelvin, yet its corona gets as hot as two million degrees. If you stand in its glare too long, your skin will turn red. Or so it will be, according to the Oracle, anyway, and she never lies."

Mischling thanked the man and moved on.

"When the Sun rises, everything on this side of the sea will turn to stone," an ostler told her. "But those who reach the far side will not. This is why the Oracle has told us to make as many boats as can be built, that all might survive the change."

"How much time is there until the Sun appears?"

"Not long," the woman said. "The Oracle has told us to finish the boats we are working on but to begin no new ones, for there will be no time to complete them."

So it went. When Mischling was done gathering information, she shared it with the brothers, concluding, "Night, they say, shall no longer be eternal, but punctuated by something called 'day.' But what that will be like, no one can say."

"What sort of thing is a boat?" Bone-Grinder asked.

"It is like a pair of shoes that allow one to stand on water and it is like a steed which will carry one across that water. It has a large cloth called a sail which gathers the wind, a stick at the back which you point at whatever direction you wish not to go, and a wheel in between which turns the stick in the opposite direction it spins."

"We must journey to the far side of the water. The new world will need guidance," said Goat-Eater.

"Therefore we require a boat large enough to hold our true forms," said Bone-Grinder, "and because this new thing, this 'sea,' will not obey our will, these people must build it for us."

The silent one made a sharp gesture.

"Or else," Bone-Grinder translated.

"But there is not enough time for them to build it," Mischling objected.

"Then we will give them time," Goat-Eater said.

The brothers raised a steep hill on the landward side of Kiv. From its heights the city was a blaze of light against the ebony sea. A galaxy of lanterns bobbed in the harbor, where boats waited to depart with the tide.

Gray and grizzled, the silent one stretched out his arm over the city. His brothers did likewise. For a long time, they were motionless. Then a rumbling arose, as if of distant artillery. Louder it grew and more thunderous, until it filled the sky and shook the land underfoot. Veins stood out on their brows and sweat poured from their faces like rain. Lightning danced about their heads. Kiv and its surroundings shimmered and blurred.

Then all was still.

Mischling, who had been holding her breath, gasped for air.

"It is done," Goat-Eater said. The brothers lowered their arms. "Kiv has been moved a decade into the past. In all that time, it will not suffer any sudden or arbitrary changes. This is a wonder such as the world has never seen."

"We still need a truth-teller," Bone-Grinder said.

The silent one pointed at Mischling.

"She will do," agreed Bone-Grinder. Seizing Mischling by her shoulders, he transfixed her with his gaze. "Every word you say, from this instant onward will be true. All who hear you will know them to be so." He released her. "Descend into the city. You will have ten years to do your work. We will return to Kiv for our boat just before its doom."

"But what do you expect me to do there?"

"You will know what to do," Goat-Eater said.

The silent one swatted her on her behind and she scampered downhill. When she looked back, the brothers were gone.

The city that Mischling entered was newer and quieter than before. Its people labored without any particular sense of urgency. Walking randomly and without purpose, she found herself in the Center Square, surrounded by guildhalls and government buildings. To one end was a platform upon which a man stood, addressing a small crowd. She climbed a set of steps on its side and shoved him out of her way. Looking down on the people, she cried, "*Hwaet!*"

She began speaking. Of the world as it was and of the world that was coming. Of the Sun and the destruction its light would bring upon them all. Of the need to build boats and to create a colony on the far side of the sea. The words came to her freely and out of nowhere. As she spoke, the crowd grew—slowly at first, and then rapidly, until the square was filled and all the streets leading into it as well. Thousands of silent faces turned up to Mischling in wonder.

When she was done speaking, the jubilant crowd hoisted Mischling to their shoulders and, cheering, paraded her through the city as if she were an idol to be adored or an effigy on its way to a burning.

For ten years, Mischling reigned in Kiv. The art of governance was not difficult since she was invariably right and all knew it. Time passed, as if in a dream—a dream in which things changed only slowly and never abruptly or arbitrarily. Her people called her the Oracle and gave her their City Hall for a dwelling place. She, in turn, devoted all her energy to the boatbuilding enterprise, so as to save as many of them as possible.

Also, she set them to building a boat that would carry three giants.

Always, in the back of her mind, Mischling pondered the brothers. They had never, she realized, chosen to give themselves wisdom. Having power, they did not need it. She, however, commanded to understand whatever she needed to understand and needing to understand everything, was well on her way to being wise.

With wisdom came judgment—and in her judgment, the new world that was coming would be far better off if she could rid it of the brothers.

But how?

One night, the Oracle was wandering her city deep in thought when a notion popped into her head. The street ahead ended in a blank storehouse wall with an alley to either side. "When I turn the corner," she said aloud, "there will be a little girl standing there, holding five kittens." Then, so as to be sure, "Horned kittens."

She turned the corner and saw a little girl struggling to control an armload of kittens. One wriggled free and the Oracle caught it as it fell. She scratched it between its nubby horns and returned it to the overburdened child. ("Thank you," said the girl. "That one's my favorite.") Then, turning back, she chose a shop at random and said, "Someone who looks exactly like Pétur will come out of that chandlery now."

A slim young man hurried out of the chandlery and for an instant Mischling's heart stopped. She had not counted on the likeness affecting her so.

"Hai-hai, Oracle!" the man said cheerily, in a voice and manner not at all like Pétur's. And was gone.

When Mischling could think calmly again, she decided to give her newly discovered power another test. She attempted to say a deliberate lie: "I was never a mouse." But she could not. No matter how she tried, the words would not form in her mouth.

This too was interesting.

The brothers had given her more power than they intended. Yet, even so, their power remained much greater than hers, and they had experience using it. Also, there were three of them and only one of her. "They will not return to Kiv," she tried to say. "They have forgotten all about their boat."

The words would not let themselves be said.

That night, lying sleepless in a bed far too large for one lone woman, Mischling found herself weeping. "I will never use this power I have selfishly," she could not say. "I will not do the terrible thing that has entered my thoughts," was also unutterable. Nor could she say, "I am strong enough to resist temptation."

It was, however, the easiest thing in the world to say: "The next time

I meet the young man who looks like Pétur, he will talk like Pétur and think like him as well." Then, since she had already gone too far, she added, "He will love me just as I love him."

That night, Mischling slept better than she had in years.

It was no coincidence that Mischling met New Pétur the next night, for immediately upon awakening, she had declared she would. But first she had to deal with a party from the Boatbuilders Guild who came to Oracle House to escort her to the yard where the Great Boat was nearing completion, so that she might inspect it.

The Great Boat was a simple klinker-built single-master, but huge beyond belief. The keel had been shaped from many large timbers doweled together, as had the strakes. The mast, similarly crafted, had to be hoisted by a crane special-built for that purpose. "It looks beautiful," the Oracle said. "Is it seaworthy?"

"I'd stake my life on it," said Katrin, the mistress of the Boatbuilders' Guild. "But . . . "

"But?"

"But we can't make a sail large enough for it."

Pushing himself forward, Einar, who was the guild's ranking mathematician, said, "Over such a large area, the first strong wind would shred it." He presented the calculations and their meaning entered the Oracle's head painlessly. "A thicker cloth might hold, but there is neither the time nor knowledge to make it."

"Have you tried sewing leather skins together?"

"The seams would not hold." Einar showed her further calculations.

"In brief," Katrin said, "all our work has been for nothing."

"A way will be found to make the sail," the Oracle said. Upon which, the answer to the problem came to her. Briefly, she was stunned by the enormity of the solution. Then she smiled in a way she could see amazed the guild-folk, for never before had they seen malice on her face. "You will build a gibbet," she said, "as tall as Oracle House and sturdy enough to hang a giant upon."

"But how will we capture this giant?" Katrin asked.

"That will not be necessary. When the time comes, he will voluntarily sacrifice himself."

So it was that, returning from the boatyard in a particularly good mood, Mischling took a sharp turn around a corner and slammed right into New Pétur. He apologized at length and, when he was done, Mischling stared silently up into his eyes. Then she took his hand and led him back to Oracle House.

Later, lying naked in a bed that no longer seemed too large for her, Mischling said, "Tell me about yourself."

"Well . . . " the so very familiar stranger said.

Pétur was a carpenter—of houses, not boats, though he could build boats as well, if called upon, and was sure he would be drafted into the boatbuilding enterprise as time ran short. He had a name, naturally, but Mischling forgot it in an instant. He also had a wife and children.

"Do you love them?" Mischling asked, fearing the answer.

"Very much," Pétur replied. "But not as much as I do you."

"Tell me about your children."

"Magnus is very young—he has just discovered how to catch one of his feet with his hands. It takes him a while to do it, but when he succeeds he looks so very pleased with himself that my heart sings. Helga is about so high, and already she is a very prim and proper little lady. If I am careless with my eating manners, she scolds me, shaking her finger at me like this!" Pétur laughed. "Oh, such children I have! I am the most fortunate father in all Kiv."

Every word made Mischling feel worse about herself. "Go back home to your children," she wanted to say, "and forget this ever happened." But what came out of her mouth was, "Tell me about your wife. But don't tell me her name."

All the light went out of Pétur. "She is a good woman, who deserves a better man than me. I thought when I married her that I would be able to keep my vows. But the heart scorns such promises. It knows only what it wants and will settle for nothing less." He was silent for a breath. "Let us talk of more pleasant matters."

So they did.

Eventually, Pétur drowsed off. Lying sleepless beside him, Mischling stared up at the ceiling. "I will send him home in the morning," she couldn't say. Nor, "A week will satisfy me." Nor, "I will not ruin his life."

In the end, the best she could manage was, "I will make up my mind when the brothers return to Kiv. If I let Pétur go, he and his family will reach the far side of the sea safely. In time, memory of me will fade. Whether his wife will ever forgive him and whether he will ever make peace with himself for the pain we are causing her, I do not know. Whether I love him enough to ever set him free, I do not know.

"But for now, he is mine."

Pétur moved into Oracle House, bringing with him a single satchel of clothes and his chest of tools. During work hours, he rehung doors, rebuilt balconies, and replaced rotting floors, for no one needed new houses.

It took no time at all for word that the Oracle had taken a married man for a lover to reach every ear in Kiv. To evil effect. Citizens—not all, but enough—concluded that there being deceit behind her actions, her words, believe them though they must, hid evil intent. Some shirked their labor; others pursued private matters at public expense, yet others refused to work at all. The boatbuilding, calculated to a nicety so there would be enough for everyone, fell behind schedule. Not all would be saved when the Sun finally rose. Worse, some of the obstructionists would be saved, while many who toiled hard and honorably wouldn't.

Pétur, who was nobody's fool, begged Mischling to send him away. "I am the cause of all this discord!"

"I cannot," she cried.

"You must."

"So long as we both love each other, I refuse to let you go."

"I don't love you."

"You lie!"

And they both knew that to be true.

Pétur's wife came to Oracle House to confront her husband's new lover. She was tall and stern, with hair as black as the look in her eyes and the hard, rough hands of a woman who has worked all her life. Under other circumstances, Mischling could have liked her quite a lot.

"I have come to take back my husband," the woman said. "He is not the man I thought he was, but his children need him and he is still mine."

Mischling put her little fists on her hips and, looking up at this big, brawny woman, said, "You have no power here and you know it."

"Do you want me to beg? Then I will beg."

"No, I want you to go. You will leave now."

The woman turned away. She had no choice. Nevertheless, over her shoulder, she said, "I'll be back."

"If you come back, your firstborn will die," Mischling said. The woman was at the door. "Come back a second time and you'll be childless." She was shouting now and almost screaming, so as to be sure she was heard, "Come back a third time and Pétur will be a widower!"

Later, with Pétur asleep beside her, Mischling stared out the window at a large red moon—there was only one moon tonight—and said aloud, "I'm as bad as the brothers. Worse, for they were never weak and don't know how it feels. I should change my name to Man-Stealer, so all the city will know my shame."

But of course they already did.

At last, the brothers returned.

Rather than put off their size, they willed the buildings to shrink away to make room for their passage. The citizens of Kiv watched in awe and fear as Mischling came out onto a balcony that Pétur had built onto Oracle House for this express purpose. Standing eye to eye with the giants, she told them what must be done if they were to have a sail for their boat. Her words did not please them. Two shouted angrily and shook their fists at her. But the third, grim and silent, turned away and plodded to the enormous gibbet at the far end of the square.

A noose was produced, woven from many ropes of normal size, and the silent one placed it about his neck.

As a mark of honor, he was hung upside down.

It took him nine hours to die.

When the deed was done, the silent one's body was taken down and flayed. Then the skin, all in one piece, was brought to a tannery to be cured prior to being made into a sail. Goat-Eater and Bone-Grinder took their brother's flayed body to the waterfront and placed it in the hold of the Great Boat, so that when they reached the far side of the sea, it might be wrapped in the sail and returned to life. For it was only on such conditions that the silent one had agreed to the sacrifice in the first place.

While the tanning and sail-making were underway, Mischling stayed as far from the surviving brothers as she could. But when the sail had been fitted onto the Great Boat, Bone-Grinder and Goat-Eater returned to Oracle Square. Mischling went out onto the balcony again. She had a plan for eliminating each of them, and clever plans they were, too. But when she opened her mouth—

"*Silence, schemer!*"

Bone-Grinder snatched up Mischling, the balcony disintegrating beneath her, and held her before his squinting eye. She could not speak. Her truth-telling had been muted. "You have worked a mighty mischief here," he said, "against one who was greater than you can imagine. You forget who—and what!—you are. Therefore, your usefulness having come to an end, be again a mouse."

In one bewildering instant, all the world loomed up around Mischling. She was all but lost in the vastness of Bone-Grinder's hand. Delicately, he set her down on the square before him. Then he raised high a foot to stamp her flat.

As that foot came crashing down, Mischling panicked and ran for the building-side. She skittered along the plinth for its partial protection. Those who had been her subjects a minute before were now giants themselves and dangers to her. Worse, she had long ago forgotten all her mouse skills. But there was an iron grate in the pavement ahead and, more by luck than intent, she fell between its bars. With a splash, she landed in stagnant water and filth. In an instant, she was back on her four feet.

She fled down the storm sewer, panting in fear.

As she fled, Mischling said to herself, "I have killed one of them and, though I am small, I will find a way to destroy the other two." She doubted the words, spoken only in her mind, had any power, particularly in her diminished form. But saying them made her feel braver. The world had no need of the brothers. Let them all die because of a mouse! Let Pétur be the cause of their downfall.

She began to make new plans.

The sewer led down to the sea. Emerging into open air onto a spill of rounded stones just above the high tide line, Mischling struggled at first to get her bearings. But the mast of the Great Boat loomed higher than anything else in the city and there was a lantern hung from its tip. She made that her lodestar.

The waterfront was all noise, lights, movement. Teamsters and stevedores were everywhere, emptying wagons and loading boats, while streams of refugees flowed about them, carrying what they could onto countless small craft. This made it difficult for Mischling to avoid being seen. But they were coming up on what the Oracle had declared would be the last outbound tide, so those who noticed Mischling had better things to do than harass a mouse. In relatively short order, she made her way to the grand pier, where an enormous hawser moored the Great Boat. It had metal baffles to keep off rodents like herself—but she had never planned to get aboard that way.

Instead, Mischling searched among the boxes and barrels to be loaded onto the Great Boat and found a crate—to her, as large as a house—where one slat had buckled, leaking a trickle of grain. The grain had a heady aroma and, nibbling a little, she felt a fraction of the power she had lost—the merest smidgen—reenter her. She squeezed between the slats, burrowing into the grain. Snug within, she wriggled around so she could look out over the waterfront and all that was happening there.

Boats were so thick on the harbor that an energetic man might cross from one side to the other by leaping from craft to craft. All who could were abandoning Kiv. Two piers over—lower and shorter and smaller piers, necessarily—Mischling saw three figures in silhouette. Two were female, tall and short, the larger one leading the smaller by her hand. The third was a man who clutched an infant to his breast. By the quickening of her heart, Mischling knew this to be New Pétur, with his family, hurrying to escape the doom about to fall on Kiv.

Mischling watched New Pétur, Magnus, Helga, and the woman whose name she had never known disappear over the edge of the pier onto a boat riding too low in the water to be seen. Hadn't she once said, back when she was the Oracle, that they would all safely reach the far side of the sea? She couldn't remember for sure. She hoped she had.

It hurt to lose her love a second time. But he was never the real Pétur anyway. Now that he was gone from her forever, she saw that she'd been a fool to behave as if he were.

Without warning, the crate Mischling was in was hurled into the sky and slammed down to the deck of the Great Boat. "That's the last of them," Bone-Grinder roared. "Let's go." He and Goat-Eater leaped onto the boat, one after the other, making it fling itself high and low, high and low.

There was a thumping of enormous boots as the boat was unmoored. "Let the sail be full of wind!" Goat-Eater commanded. "Brother, take the wheel and put Kiv to our backs. We must be on the far side of the sea before the rising of the Sun."

Water began to rush past the hull.

"Let the city of Kiv burn behind us," Bone-Grinder rumbled, "so that we always know which direction to steer away from." In the wake of his words there came a roaring noise from landward, as of an all-consuming conflagration, and shortly thereafter the stench of burning buildings.

Their escape from oncoming doom had put the brothers in a good mood. "What should we do first when we reach the new land?" asked one. (Burrowing deeper into the grain, Mischling could not tell which muffled voice was which.) "Create bronze idols of ourselves to be worshipped? Change the mountains to rivers and the swamps to glaciers? Kill all the survivors of the old land and create new ones to replace them?"

"All these things we shall do," said the other, "just as soon as we have restored our brother to life. And much more as well."

The words made Mischling's blood run cold.

Nevertheless, she slipped out of her sanctuary crate. Mischling no longer had the Oracle's power to reshape the world, nor a woman's strength with which to sabotage the boat. But she had sharp little teeth.

Also, she knew the Great Boat's construction, from top to bottom.

The boat's wheel turned ropes that ran through pulleys below the deck to port and starboard, then back through a second set of pulleys to a spindle that made the rudder turn in the direction opposite the wheel's rotation. In this counterintuitive manner, the boat could be turned in the same direction as the wheel.

Mischling crept below, undetected.

Overhead, Goat-Eater and Bone-Grinder boasted, laughed, wrestled, and sang songs. They knew just enough to sail the boat. However, because they had never needed to understand how things work, they could never repair the tiller mechanism should it break. They would be left adrift at sea.

As would she. But that was a price Mischling was willing to pay for the sake of all who managed to escape the old country of perpetual night. Also, it might serve to atone, in part, for what she had done to New Pétur and his family.

The seas were calm and the course steady. Mischling climbed atop one of the ropes—it was many times thicker than she—that connected wheel and rudder. She anchored herself with all eighteen claws.

She began to gnaw.

The most heroic deeds are often drab and boring. Mischling attacked the rope with her teeth, to little effect. But she kept slashing, gnawing, and nibbling for hour after hour. Her jaws grew weary, then sore, and then numb. When she had made an inroad into the rope large enough for her to crawl into it, she stopped to examine her work. Whichever brother was at the wheel gave it a jerk and the rope *leaped*. Climbing back up, Mischling eyed the damaged rope carefully to see if it gave any sign of being ready to part.

It did not.

With an imagined sigh, she got back to work.

Up top, the brothers took turns at the wheel, with occasional breaks to gamble at dice or argue or piss over the side, during which the Great Boat went wherever it listed.

Meanwhile, Mischling kept gnawing away, like the Worm at the roots of the world tree said by some to exist at the northernmost pole of the world. Time and again, it came on her that the task was hopeless. Over and over, she thought of reasons to quit. Still, she persisted. This is my punishment, she thought, for acting like one of the mighty. But if punishment it was, it was one she accepted, for she did not stop gnawing.

Then a single strand of rope fiber popped straight up from where she'd been chewing.

Mischling stopped, blinked. A second strand popped up.

The rope quivered like a violin string.

The brothers were banging about overhead, unaware of this new peril. Looking up through the hatchway for the first time since she had started severing the rope, Mischling saw that the sky was lighter than any she had ever known. The words *false dawn* popped into her head, and though she did not know their meaning, they gave her hope. She strained to make sense of the brothers' voices.

"It's coming! We must make speed or . . . "

"We're almost there. Look! There on the . . . it's rising up!"

"Not a . . . too soon. Our only chance . . . "

Mischling scurried to find a place directly under the brothers, where she could hear them with greatest clarity. This was made more difficult by the way their voices rose and fell and overlapped. But she thought she had found it when—

The rope broke.

Its two halves lashed back and forth like bullwhips, hissing in the air. Mischling cowered beneath them. She heard the brothers shout in anger and amazement. Goat-Eater tumbled down below like a rockslide and, seeing the flying ropes, seized first one and then the other. Cursing, he tied the two of them together. But in doing so, he yanked out the pulleys they rode in. So when he lumbered back up, he found the wheel still slack and the boat unwilling to obey it.

Mischling, meanwhile, followed in Goat-Eater's shadow and found a hiding place within a stack of crates and sacks where, unobserved, she could watch her plan play out.

"Look!" cried Bone-Grinder, pointing one long, misshapen arm to the east. "It comes!"

A golden line of color touched the horizon, harbinger of the coming Sun. In that direction lay the mountains and forests and cities of the old country, doubtless already turned to stone. Before them, the dark cliffs of the new country loomed up. "We must reach land," cried Goat-Eater. "But the boat refuses to obey me."

"We are almost there," answered Bone-Grinder. "Grab the rope and leap overboard. We can pull the boat to shore."

There was a splash and then another. Mischling emerged from the shadows and climbed up on the rail. The land was so very close, only minutes away. There was no doubt in her mind that the brothers would reach it.

She wanted to cry.

But then, with a radiance that was like the fanfare of a thousand trumpets, the Sun breasted the horizon. Its light stretched out across the sea to touch the Great Boat and the brothers pulling it. The boat and then the brothers slowed, stilled, turned to stone. The black stone rope connecting the three broke into a hundred fragments and fell into the sea, there to begin the ages-long process of turning into sand.

To her surprise, Mischling did not turn to stone. In all the Great Boat, she was the only thing that didn't. Why this should be, she did not know, unless it was that she was too small and unimportant for such a grand transformation. She felt inside herself for her lost power and found that a small fragment of it lingered.

Summoning that power, Mischling changed herself back to a woman. She stripped out of her clothes. Then she slipped over the boat's stony side and swam toward shore. When she was on solid land, she would decide whether to be mouse or maid.

And then she would give herself a new name.

Three sea stacks stand just off the black sand beach Reynisfjara near the village of Vik on the southern coast of Iceland. Legend has it that they are two trolls and a boat they were hauling to shore, all turned to stone when they were caught by the rays of the rising sun. This is the first and only true account of what actually occurred. Let all who read these words be schooled thereby and live their lives accordingly.

ABOUT THE AUTHOR

Michael Swanwick is one of the most acclaimed and prolific science fiction and fantasy writers of his generation. He is the recipient of the Nebula, Theodore Sturgeon, and World Fantasy Awards as well as five Hugo Awards.

This year's *The Iron Dragon's Mother,* completes a trilogy begun twenty-five years before with *The Iron Dragon's Daughter.* Out even more recently is *City Under the Stars,* a novel co-authored with the late Gardner Dozois.

He lives in Philadelphia with his wife, Marianne Porter.

Conversations in the Dark

ROBERT REED

1

An absence of visible light: that was the first goal and easily accomplished. But true darkness—profound; enduring; seamless—meant excluding the rest of the electromagnetic spectrum, or masking it, or otherwise rendering it inconsequential. Windowless walls, ceiling, and floor were built from plates of radiologically stable graphene. Hyperfiber boxes and long reaches of frigid vacuum further isolated the chamber, while multiple faraday cages killed the influx of long-wave radiation. And the little dribbles that seeped past those barricades were artfully poisoned with a stew of EM antinoise, creating a faint gray Nothing.

All this was a worthwhile beginning.

But echolocation couldn't be allowed. Or touching surfaces, since subtle vibrations might give the occupant clues about the interrogators. To solve those challenges, perfluorocarbon was mixed with synthetic bloods inspired by cetacean-class aliens. The result was a blackish fluid, where density and thermal properties could be adjusted as needed. Set adrift, the creature would be steered to the center of the chamber and made to hover in place. If oxygen was necessary for life, the gas would be dissolved in the perfluorocarbon and then delivered to the lungs or gills or an intricately folded rectum. To maintain the metabolism, wide varieties of foodstuffs could be synthesized on-site, then injected. There would be no flavor, no joy. In effect, they wanted to build the most elaborate sensory deprivation chamber in human history.

Yet grand accomplishments meant little if outside eyes could observe the facility. And layers of camouflage, inert as well as active, would accomplish only so much. That's why obscure, hard-to-reach locations were identified, then rejected. The logic was that potential adversaries would build similar lists, and that's why every obvious candidate had to be avoided.

Lowering the benchmarks. That was the only workable answer.

"Smarter to do the unexpected," was the more hopeful logic.

A billion subpar hiding locations were put into a common pool, the final choice made by random means.

Next, purpose-built drones began construction, which was finished in a mere thirty years.

From outside, there was nothing to see but a pillar of structural hyperfiber, unblemished and as old as the Great Ship.

While inside, pure perfect darkness waited.

2

Voussoir and her squad were walking the F'Tar District. The populace was mostly KillarTwos, nocturnal as well as instinctively allergic to authority, which was why the bright midday avenues were largely empty. Boredom was the enemy today, and being experienced soldiers, the eight of them cherished the drudgery while hoping for something bright and violent around the next bend.

What came for them were encrypted commands from the high echelons. The squad was to disarm itself immediately, disable every nexus and blind the sensors woven into their uniforms, then climb inside a waiting cap-car.

The subsequent journey should have proved quick, except random turns and security portals meant that a full hour passed, and that's why the squad napped in shifts, four at a time.

Voussoir woke up male.

This seq-herm's shifting of sex began in adolescence, one hundred and six centuries ago, and not once had that celebration of potential repeated itself precisely. Body mass was constant, minus what was lost to satisfy the fierce metabolic demands. But the face always shifted features around the appealingly androgynous template. Height varied a little or quite a lot, while muscle and fat shifted proportions and placement. And though the skin was a constant blue-black, the scalp grew a different crop of hair ranging from snow to anthracite, downy fine to bristly thick.

This day's transformation proved exceptionally lean, powerful, and swift. And because instinct occasionally shaped the next body, Voussoir tugged at the new blonde curls, joking about how he must be getting ready for war.

The squad laughed with their lieutenant while silently battling superstitions.

The cap-car finally arrived at its berth inside a secure garage, opening up to reveal, of all people, the head of Ship Security. Marshall G was a robust figure, stern mannered but loved by his soldiers for not being the considerable asshole that his predecessor had been. He had a square face and a pale purple cast to the skin, one natural eye that saw quite a lot, while the augmented eye was rumored to peer deep into his soldiers' souls.

G stared only at the lieutenant.

Salutes were offered and roundly ignored, as were quizzical gazes and a thousand obvious questions floating silently about them. Then the moment was done, and both the black uniform and the purple man turned and walked away, no words worth saying to lowly troops.

Voussoir and his squad marched behind their superior. The garage was part of an expansive field station that felt new, yet was neglected by names or a posted location. Pulses of radiation kept pouring through their bodies, searching . . . for what? Guarded hatches led deeper into a sequence of nested faraday structures, and then this crazed security culminated with a final sealed chamber where no guard stood.

Touching the last door, Marshall G stepped back again.

"Not us," he said. "Just you."

Voussoir, he meant.

One last glance was offered to his comrades. "Better you than me," was what the familiar faces said to him. Then that warrior's body summoned the courage to take the next few steps.

The room beyond smelled of smoke, which was entirely reasonable, lit as it was by a few dozen tall wax candles. Several Submasters were seated in a row, while the infamous First Chair, Miocene, stood before them. Everything about the scene was surprising, borderline crazy, and would the lords of the Great Ship mind if Voussoir burst into laughter? He was ready to out-and-out giggle. But then he noticed the bulky object to his left, and turning just his head, he saw the Master Captain stretched out on a mattress. Sleeping, by the looks of it. Unless she was dead.

But no, those ancient lungs were breathing just fine.

All at once, Voussoir wished he was even stronger and faster. As if that might help with whatever was about to transpire.

"Where you are," Miocene began.

Then she paused.

Voussoir took a stance that could be held for days. Feet apart, forearms horizontal at the waist, elbows cradled by the opposite hands.

There was a barracks joke where the First Chair began existence as an old-fashioned surgical knife, but then an evil doctor made the knife live, though neglecting to add kindness or any passion. That's why Miocene looked like she did, narrow-faced and ready to cut. That's why every member of the Ship's crew feared her gaze or the sound of their names riding her voice. Yet in that curious human manner, people often craved attention from the Great Ship's immortal second-in-command.

"The Vermiculate," said Miocene.

"That's where we are," Voussoir presumed.

"Do you know it?"

"Never been stationed here, madam. But I've hiked a few rooms while on leave. Desiccated, dark, unpopulated. And huge. With all its twists and cubbies, no other labyrinth inside the Great Ship is half as complicated. Or so I understand."

While Voussoir spoke, Miocene offered nods. Then as soon as he stopped, she asked, "Are you aware? Several belief systems claim that the Vermiculate isn't just a random mess of spongelike stone and hyperfiber. Some local minds insist on believing that these knotted up tunnels and odd rooms create an alien text. A topological language is at work here, and if you can look at the Vermiculate in the proper manner, clarity waits beyond the randomness. Deep meanings want to be found inside the chaos. At least that's what the enthusiasts promise."

"I've heard the claims," he said. "But I don't believe any of it, madam."

"No?"

"Metaphysical thunder," he said, laughing scornfully. But that wasn't enough of a dismissal. "It's my basic policy, madam. Respect no voice that lacks the courage to step up and make itself heard clearly."

That wrung laughter out of the First Chair. "A fair point," she conceded, glancing at the slumbering bulk warmed by candlelight.

"I assume the Master is healthy, madam."

"Our subject is the Vermiculate," Miocene replied. Then she stared at the soldier, black eyes catching the dancing candle fires. "Officially, this region was successfully mapped, as was the rest of the Great Ship, and that happened at the very beginning. Self-cloning scouts crawled through every entranceway, memorizing surfaces while probing hidden chambers. Wherever a tunnel split, they reproduced. Bodies grew smaller but the army became ever larger, fifty generations relentlessly sharing data with one another. Nothing was missed here, certainly nothing of consequence, and that's why we remained confident. But as I've mentioned, certain passengers and a few gullible crew members regard this grotto as a mystery. A challenge. Then add to the chorus some persistent AI voices who live for no reason but to distract the Master with unlikely unpalatables."

Miocene paused, stepping closer to Voussoir. "Of course, the unlikely does love to become real, at least now and again. For example, some recently massaged data convinced our mapmakers that a miniscule portion of the Vermiculate had evaded detection. Some intriguing factors suggest why this had happened. But you don't need to know the reasons. The critical point is that a tiny problem existed, and to cure it, I ordered advanced, highly competent scouts set into motion.

"Most returned with news about little rooms, all empty. But one scout managed to lose its way—an astonishing development for a device designed for no purpose but cartography.

"In the end, disgusted engineers recovered the machine and tore it apart. And nothing was wrong. Not physically, not with its resident software. No, the only oddity was its failed job, and too, a foreign item found inside the machine's body, placed there by unknown hands.

"There's no good reason to share the technical peculiarities with you. A thorough briefing would take far too much time. All you need to know is this: inside the machine, we found a babble-pocket of an entirely unfamiliar design. Despite multiple attempts, the pocket refused to open for us. But it helpfully explained itself. 'I have words for the Master Captain,' it claimed. The voice was human, male, and it used the Ship's standard tongue. 'I demand an audience with the Master Captain.' And that's why after considerable analysis and several layers of additional security, I personally carried the troublemaker to the Master, and she said to it, 'I'm here, now tell me what's so important.'

"The same voice that spoke to us spoke to the Captain. But instead of ship standard, it used an archaic, entirely unexpected language."

And with that, Miocene fell silent.

"Madam," said Voussoir.

Today's voice was rumbling and slow.

"Yes, Lieutenant?"

"This is ridiculously interesting. But I fail to see why we're here, madam."

His tone was assertive and prickly, and in other circumstances that might earn a reflexive dressing down from superiors. But Miocene was one the rulers of the Great Ship. To her, everyone else was tiny, complaints were harmless noise, and Voussoir felt protected by his utter lack of station.

"You've been ordered here," she said, "because the Master has been invited to meet with someone. Or nobody will be waiting for her, and a joke is being played on us. Either way, a small chamber waits half a kilometer from us. To our knowledge, the chamber has never been physically entered. Not by humans or our scouts, or any other species or machines. But we have studied the site from a distance. Nothing is inside it, and we have zero evidence that any creature will appear there. Yet the Master has been summoned, and in the best spirit possible, the Master will make her appearance."

"My squad supplies security," Voussoir said doubtfully.

"If guards had been invited, she'd bring women and men already known to her. But no, the babble-pocket had instructions to share. Nobody but the Master Captain will be welcome."

Once more, Voussoir looked at the sleeping woman. An enormous human, physically as well through her considerable reach, her rounded body held fleets of nexuses, each one of those sophisticated machines constantly absorbing data and churning out instructions. Which made her a target to all of the Ship's enemies, naturally, and that's why she had to be protected at all costs.

Voussoir was far from an expert in this rarified paranoia, but one response was obvious.

"Someone has built an obvious trap," he stated. "So why the hell bother?"

"Let me reiterate," Miocene said. "The chamber and its surroundings have been studied. Sonics. Gamma blades. Neutrino pulses and gravimetric maps. If an entity waits there, we cannot see it. And if it hides that well, it could be anywhere else. For instance, standing between us right now, invisible and wickedly amused."

Ever so slightly, Voussoir flinched.

"Multiple precautions are in place," Miocene promised. "We're ready to abuse but never entirely break the terms of this meeting. For example, the rest of your squad will be armed with kinetics and shock weapons, and they'll escort the captains' captain to her destination, deploying in depth. The chamber has a single entrance. Unless a second tunnel hides, but let's ignore that impossibility. Your squad's assignment will be simple. Should anyone other than the Master follow them into the hole or try to escape from the hole, they will maim the creature without killing it, or they'll die trying to halt its progress."

A silent moment passed.

Then the long back straightened even more than normal, and with appealing certainty, Miocene said, "Everything is unknown, including the specific hazards. But this day may help the Great Ship, perhaps in some essential, unexpected way, and that's why the mission is necessary."

The other Submasters climbed to their feet.

Before all of those gods of authority, Lieutenant Voussoir bowed deeply. Then to the First Chair, he said, "My apologies, madam. But I don't understand."

"What confounds you, my boy?"

"My squad guards the doorway, but what am I to do?"

Disappointment arrived with a sigh and a slow shake of the face. Then Miocene walked over the sleeping Master, and with one captain's boot, she kicked that huge belly.

Untroubled, the carcass continued breathing.

"Oh shit," Voussoir said. "Oh goddamn shit."

3

While the babble-pocket and Master spoke, Marshall G stood at a respectful distance. His presence had been deemed crucial, but not for security concerns, since the captains already had every tool and instinct available to their warriors. No, as the ranking security officer, G served as one more precaution and a very generous nod to tradition. The Great Ship had always been a civilian vessel. That was why mirrored uniforms would forever outrank black uniforms. The Marshall's office was reserved for those who had served the Master with quiet distinction, and the symbolic honor rarely lasted more than five or six centuries.

G had been briefed about the plan to remap the Vermiculate, and later, when the babble-pocket was discovered, the Submasters included him in the investigations, inviting insights and recommendations.

After which they acted exactly as they wanted to act all along.

"I am here," the Master Captain declared. "Now tell me what's so important."

The babble-pocket had a pleasantly masculine voice—one detail that may or may not have been calculated to win over the ancient lady. But instead of using the Ship's standard tongue, as before, it employed obscure, long-dead human phonetics: Khoisan from southern Africa, with modifications to allow for modern terminology. Clicks and pops came from what pretended to be a human tongue and human throat, and a linguistic AI fed translations to the wary audience.

"Ah, the grand mistress of us all," the little machine began. Then it laughed in the most impolite way, the tone neither comforting nor friendly.

When the laughter ceased, the voice returned.

"I am here to tell you about some grave dangers thriving under your foolish toes."

In the standard tongue, the Master said, "My toes are interested in whatever you have to share."

The babble-pocket responded with a story about Pcici traders smuggling antimatter slivers. Captains and Marshall G knew about the situation, but the mechanical informant added several helpful details, including the present whereabouts of the operation's leader.

The Marshall dispatched troops to the dragnet.

Noticing those orders, Miocene said nothing to G, thus giving her full blessing.

"Thank you for that news," the Master was saying. Then with a put-upon tone, she added, "How many more hazards are there?"

"Two that I am free to mention," it promised.

First came tales of a multispecies cult that was plotting to hijack a district and form its own nation. Captains and Security alike were disgusted, and combing reconnaissance logs, Miocene found enough evidence to order the Marshall to prepare strike forces.

Through two nexuses, G gave the go-aheads for a micro-war while also insulting certain talents inside his Intelligence services.

"Make up for this blunder," he demanded from his trip wires. "Find me ten more plots. By tomorrow."

Then the third hazard was offered, which proved much, much worse than the others. An AI savant had secretly gone mad, broken its safeguards, and its genius was now planning the murder of every other savant serving the captains' ranks.

The Master interrupted.

"I don't believe you."

Babble-pockets were far more than audio files. Reactive and astute, this device giggled as it said, "But you do believe me. Being human, you have no other choice but accept every word that is absorbed, and only afterward, if you remember to, will you unleash your doubts."

Glancing at her First Chair, the Master said, "Let me examine this trouble."

"You will find it valid. But yes, grand mistress. I will wait here while appropriate inquiries are made."

Inquiries led to incontrovertible evidence. Yet this unfolding disaster was aimed at the captains, and no one considered the Marshall's help. On an encrypted river, Miocene called to a captain who had been one of the Ship's sterling engineers, giving her authority and nearly infinite resources. G's only role was to help search for signs that the disembodied voice might have been involved in any these schemes. But nothing was found. The Ship was already full of smugglers and cults, and dangerous AIs certainly didn't need any help from simple babble-pockets.

In prudence, G advised Miocene to pause the interview for a day or a few years.

The First Chair listened to him or ignored him. Either way, she nodded to the Master, the gesture meaning, "Go on."

"All right," said the captains' captain. "Continue."

"But I have so little left to share," it said. "There is just one more hazard, a fourth treachery that is infinitely larger than any sabotage or genocide. But I can't share any of the specifics."

"Why not?"

"Because I know nothing." The mocking laugh returned. "He who made me made me ignorant."

"You said, 'Infinitely larger,'" the Master quoted.

"The foe is that, yes."

"So you're assuming that much. And maybe you hold an intuition or instinct about what this means."

The pocket made agreeable sounds.

"What I assume," it said, "is that the Great Ship is the warning's subject. My intuition thinks that after all these years of criminal ignorance, you are about to see your vast machine with new eyes. And most importantly, instinct keeps insisting that you need to hear why your species controls the most valuable property in the universe."

Over the last few centuries, Marshall G had spent much time with the Master Captain, and his impression was that few creatures were more immune to surprise or less likely to act impressed than she was.

Yet at that point, the Master sighed. Shivered. Then she seemingly misplaced her voice.

"Much needs to be learned," said the pocket. "But you gain these lessons only if you, the present ruler of the Great Ship, can make yourself walk into a specific hole. Which is *here*."

A precise location was delivered.

And detailed instructions about what was permitted and what was forbidden.

After which, the babble-pocket never spoke again.

Marshall G never agreed to this mysterious meeting. He spoke against it at the outset, in every available public way. "The captains' captain remains on the bridge, and we send an AI facsimile," he proposed to the Submasters. "Or one of you goes in her place. Or we melt the Vermiculate and bottle up the slag wreckage. Though the best solution, I'd argue, is ignoring, denying, forgetting, and moving on."

"Perhaps you should be the one to meet our mysterious informant," Miocene mentioned.

"If ordered, I'll go," he replied.

An obvious bluff, and it served its purpose. Public debates were declared finished. The First Chair and the Master spoke privately to one another—a never-ending conversation already a thousand centuries old. Then that vast, ancient, and often wise mind uttered the command it always intended to give.

"I will go into that empty room and say 'Hello,'" she declared.

Most of the Submasters squirmed with pain.

Only Miocene smiled. Then turning, focusing on the Marshall, she said, "But we have a work-around. There's another possibility . . . that I neglected to mention to you, somehow . . . "

4

Changing gender took no time. Everyone born into the Family of Perpetual Renewal had that talent. Restructuring the body was much more involved and expensive, but then again, modern tissues were immortal, and with energy reserves and its native powers of healing, the healthy body could do considerable work in just twenty furious minutes.

Among the first human passengers to board the Great Ship, the Family of Perpetual Renewal were committed to spreading their goodness across the Milky Way. But terraforming worlds required wealth and sacrifice, and when those blessings were exhausted, the Family lost their calling and quit living together as organized communities. Many customs died, but "Voussoir" was a name still bestowed to every generation. This particular Voussoir was born in an obscure district. Childhood was full of concessions and tempered aspirations, but the poverty wasn't nearly enough to make anyone bitter. Home was only forty rooms, but they were comfortable rooms. Human mouths were scarce along the local avenues, and that was why this Voussoir grew up accustomed to alien bodies and biologies, including a mating ensemble of Jick'ick'mee—half a hundred bipeds with little money, no significance to the Ship, and a history of intraspecies violence.

Voussoir was still a genderless child when they saw their first corpse. The victim—a Jick'ick'mee male—had died inside an alcove where the young human often built forts and starships. Voussoir discovered the corpse but didn't understand what they had found. They were that young, that ridiculously innocent. Because the fellow was lying on his back, breathing slowly, he had to be asleep or enjoying a drugged state. The neighbor most certainly looked the same as he did just yesterday. Jick'ick'mee were beautiful creatures, orange fur tipped with snow, long faces and long eyes and voices that sang best in their own language, which they preferred over the Ship's standard tongue.

Voussoir often played alone, but this day had delivered a companion who didn't care what the human child did or said, and that was a blessing. All morning, Voussoir pretended they were the captain of a streakship and the alien was their crew. Orders were given. Intricate scenarios were built on top of one another. Not one but several attacks were made against the streakship, but Voussoir and their loyal crew fended off a sequence of fierce, poorly defined enemies.

Eventually their father came looking for them.

Father was a woman that day.

She began by asking, "What are you two doing?"

Then in the middle of the explanation, she called out the man's name.

But sleep was too precious, it seemed. Their beautiful neighbor left his eyes closed, refusing to wake.

Father kneeled, and for the third time in Voussoir's brief, amazing life, they saw one of their parents praying.

That alone was reason to ask, "What's wrong, my ancestor?"

How to explain murder to a child? That was a question asked behind sad eyes. Then the day's voice told a lie. "Your friend isn't here, Voussoir. Someone stole away his mind, as a joke."

Except this wasn't a theft or joke. An illegal plasma torch had vaporized flesh and skull and the bioceramic machinery inside, after which the immortal body did its best to heal the wound, producing an empty but otherwise flawless head. But parents were to be believed, and that's why the child accepted the explanation. Several confusing, embarrassing days passed before they finally learned the truth, and that was one of many reasons why Voussoir despised anyone who hid behind soft words and hopeful lies.

Modern human minds were built on a nearly universal template, their perfection delivering relentless memories that could reach across ten thousand years.

The grown security officer stared at the Master Captain's body, muttering, "Oh shit. Oh goddamn shit."

Anticipating one train of thought, Miocene said, "But this isn't Her. The Master Captain is healthy and whole."

In other words, "I haven't murdered my superior, and you're not entangled in mutiny."

But even so, the situation was extraordinary. Stealing away the Master Captain's mind meant disabling or fooling every native security system, and that was just the first hurdle. Outside eyes couldn't notice the work occurring, and presumably that's why the carcass was still full of busy nexuses spitting out commands. What's more, the intricate work had to be finished quickly, with only a tiny few people in-the-know.

Of course if anyone could manage that impossible task, it was the Master's loyal First Chair.

Voussoir knelt. The sleeping face was exactly like the Master's old face. Minus personality, presence, or even the beginnings of a voice.

Submasters gathered behind him, no doubt trading opinions through shielded nexuses.

"Timetable?" Voussoir asked.

Miocene offered several hours for the surgery and minimal adjustments.

"You're assuming I'll respond better than most," the lieutenant guessed. "Since I change bodies daily and all."

"One positive trait among several, yes," Miocene said.

"What else?"

"Your natural voice is blunt. Rather like hers."

Voussoir rose and turned, very slightly bowing to his superiors. "And you noticed this when, madam? A few days ago?"

"No, there's always been a stand-in scenario, and you topped the candidate list several thousand years ago."

Voussoir managed a tight laugh.

"One duty of the First Chair," said Miocene, "is to make ready for the unlikely, the barely imaginable."

Another glance at the empty carcass seemed like enough.

Then staring at the chamber's gray ceiling, Voussoir asked, "Does Marshall G know what you're planning?"

"Yes. But no one else in Security."

Of course not. Captains trusted captains with their secrets, and almost nobody else. "If this is a trap, and there's an assassination attempt, I'll likely be dead in another few hours."

"Almost certainly so."

No, Miocene never softened her messages.

Voussoir bowed low, and with honest respect, she said. "No more talking, madam. Bring in an autodoc, and let's get the hacking done."

5

Voussoir had been swallowed up by candlelight, and turning to the rest of the squad, Marshall G gave explicit orders: they would never speak about this place or this day, and that included casual words shared between one another. Rare punishments were promised, obscure laws quoted, face and voice delivering the news with a rich mixture of duty and disgust. Then with that necessary housekeeping finished, the briefing finally began.

Except what they were told proved so slender, so totally inadequate, that every soldier asked, "Who the hell is telling this joke?"

They asked the question with offended faces, offended stances, the doubled-up fists. But never words.

On its surface, the assignment couldn't have been simpler. Their lieutenant wasn't here because he had a separate job, undefined, but the easy assumption put Voussoir inside a secure bunker, watching over them with extra ordnance. Which was a soothing image. Without their lieutenant, the rest would take posts inside a very ordinary passageway, watching the most important creature on the Ship march out of sight. After that, some alien or ghost or nothing at all would speak to the old lady. Every soldier took "nothing" as the only viable option. The mysterious chamber had never been seen or touched, but that didn't make it invisible. Exceptional sensors had surrounded the pit and found nobody lurking inside, and that had to be the truth. Otherwise a soldier's imagination might lead to monsters—organic creatures, untethered AIs, or some wicked hybrid of the two. Imagination was a tireless enemy. Imagination invited distraction and surprise, and suppose that every sensor was wrong. Suppose a physical entity lurked inside that nameless hole. Then when trouble comes, the soldier reacts with useless expectations, slowing her reaction times.

Every soldier wore battle armor with cannons on hips, and towing sensors and camouflage arrays, they assembled before a freshly constructed hatchway. Then they waited, and waited. The notoriously punctual Master arrived several minutes late, and not only that, she seemed peculiarly distracted.

Without Voussoir, Sister-Witch held command. With a respectful but serious voice, she begged the Master to step back please, allowing her and two of her people to take the lead. And not only did she do as told, but with a nervous nod, as if saying, "Whatever you think best."

Sister-Witch wasn't the most experienced soldier here, but she was twice the age of the next oldest. That's why Voussoir made her his

Second. "You had careers and lives before this career and life, and that's perfect training for walking corridors with every kind of everyone."

Relishing responsibility, Sister-Witch deployed a diamond shield and fed it orders, and when the shield advanced, she followed in its wake. Cumbersome gear demanded considerable room. The shield was fifty meters down the passageway before the Master finally stepped past the hatchway, and then the final four soldiers followed with their munitions, armor, and paranoid sensors. Every sentient weapon knew its stopping point. The winding tunnel was saturated with antinoise and a wicked super-mint odor designed to baffle average nostrils. Native granite formed the walls and the rolling floor and a rather low ceiling. Humans had never come this way before. Only microchine scouts had been sent, and according to a ghost's strict rules, those scouts moved only so far. But there were so many ways to make rock transparent. Not one flake of left-behind skin had been discovered, not one spent breath lingered against the ceiling, and the thin dust introduced by billions of years of neglect was undisturbed even by the feet of a harum-scarum flea.

Sister-Witch had never knowingly visited such pristine ground, and when her anxieties ebbed, she found herself feeling honored.

One hundred meters walked, and then another hundred, and two of her people stopped walking, setting up barricades and all-spectrum eyes while the rest of the squad continued into the dark little hole.

This had to be the most ludicrous day in Creation. What began as unlikely mutated into the ridiculous, with insanity happy to rear its grinning face. How could the Master agree to this crap? And why wouldn't Miocene—a notoriously competent officer—forbid this "meeting" from occurring? Indeed, why not lock up the Vermiculate, fill it with poisons, then for extra measure, throw the troublesome babble-pocket into a blazing Ship engine?

The second pair of soldiers deployed.

Then the third, but only after allowing the Master to squeeze past them.

Sensible reasons put Sister-Witch on point, prepared to take the forward post or the last post. Her duty was to cripple whatever was hiding beyond, should it try to escape, or if some malevolence approached from outside, show it a last-ditch fight after the rest of her people were dead.

Her working plan was to stop on one stretch of stone rock, exactly where the tunnel began a last soft turn. But reaching that point, the squad leader thought again. Three steps beyond felt better. Who the hell knew why?

Stopping there, she stepped out of the way, beckoning to the giant who was slowly approaching from behind.

Just then, the Master Captain hesitated. A bioluminescent torch floated before her, revealing the famous face, dark smart eyes almost lost against rounded flesh and bone.

"The shield stays with you," said Sister-Witch.

"Thank you," the famous voice replied.

"You're welcome, madam. The best fortune to you."

The diamond shield had gone ahead, and the torch seemed eager to do the same.

Again, the Master said, "Thank you."

Then she walked past.

Too late, Sister-Witch thought of touching the ancient, oversized lady. On the wrist, perhaps. Or patting her broad back. Either gesture would have made this remarkable day even better, enjoying some small but friendly contact, bare fingers against the mirrored uniform that every captain wore in official circumstances.

But the ancient woman and her light were already vanishing into the black ink, and concluding once more that nobody was waiting inside the hole, Sister-Witch promised herself that the Master Captain would soon return, and regardless of the lady's response—elation or despair or any state between—this loyal warrior would grab her with both hands, if only just to know how it feels to be so close to such vast, enduring power.

6

A difficult surgery was finished, and not only that, it had been done in a rush, needing only a few intense, remarkable hours.

First, Voussoir was shoved into dreamless sleep, then his mind was knitted into the empty body. Cold pain woke him next, and feeling male again, he thought of apologizing and tried to sit up. The giant body refused to obey, but one arm let itself rise off the operating table. Eyes not as sharp as his old eyes examined the hand's wide palm and fat fingers. Fingers moved as he willed, which might be a good sign. But he still couldn't sit upright, and while his mouth opened and closed again, it refused to say sensible words. Which was why he shoved two fingers and the thumb between the jaws, yanking at the useless tongue.

Someone grabbed the wrist.

Miocene said, "Sleep again."

Next time, Voussoir woke as a female.

But something else was amiss, or unfinished, and she was forced back under as the work progressed.

Twenty-three naps; twenty-three instantaneous transformations.

Then she was completely awake, and standing beside the surgical table, Miocene said, "All right. Try the voice."

"You planned this doppelgänger bullshit," said Voussoir.

"As an emergency measure. As I mentioned—"

Voussoir interrupted. "With me. Me. Centuries and centuries ago, you stuck me in your plans. Just in case."

Delight emerged as a fleeting smile, sharp and then gone again. "Maybe, yes. Maybe I found you earlier than implied. And maybe that's why Security recruiters approached you even before you were grown."

The revelation deserved silence and some hard considerations.

"Sit up," the First Chair urged.

Better than that, Voussoir threw the giant legs over the table's edge, then stood tall.

Miocene was tiny beside her.

The Master's body was a graceful mass. Bending at the waist, Voussoir grabbed the First Chair's hands and kissed their backs lightly. Then with a quiet voice, she said, "I apologize to you, madam."

"For what?"

"I've heard that you're a marvel of frigid genius. A puppet master of the highest order. But I never appreciated your magnificence, madam . . . "

A briefing about practical matters included what to expect inside the never-seen chamber, and Voussoir was given a few minutes to practice with the new body, achieving some sense of normalcy. A second, much more thorough briefing offered goals if this "meeting" became real. What to ask, what to watch for and learn. Likely subjects, less likely subjects, and what issues to avoid by every possible means. All of those instructions came inside a rush of moments and deep breaths, and Voussoir was left more alert than she had ever felt before . . . besides those few times of honest combat.

She'd rather fight war than endure this crap again.

She asked a few obvious questions, breaking the briefings' momentum, and when they were well behind schedule, Miocene said, "We're done. Go."

With the Master's borrowed voice, Voussoir said, "You should have allowed for more minutes, madam."

"Next time, I will."

What followed was painfully long and banal. Voussoir walked with her unaware squad, or the seven of them had been briefed in full and were pretending ignorance. Or maybe they could see through the subterfuge, and on their own, they were doing a stellar job of maintaining the lie.

Regardless, she was proud of them, so much so she ached.

Then Sister-Witch was standing guard, and Voussoir walked alone until the tunnel decided to end its existence, opening into a hollow space that looked exactly as expected: a volume not much bigger than a comfortable bedroom, the space defined by ordinary granite, ordinary air. There was silence when she was silent, and besides herself, nobody else was present.

"Of course nothing's waiting for me," she told herself.

She filled the Master's lungs and held that breath, exhausting the oxygen, letting modern anaerobic metabolisms come online. Most of the nexuses inside her—armies of self-absorbed talent—had been disabled or dropped into diagnostic modes. The exceptions served as eyes and ears absorbing every input. That's what the genuine Master Captain would have done in these circumstances. This was reasonable security coupled with heightened senses. Voussoir's only companion was the silent torch, and for twenty minutes, nothing changed. For another thirteen seconds, nothing changed. Then following Miocene's script, she used the Master's voice to say, "Enough," and took one long step backward.

The torch went out. Or perhaps, her new eyes were stricken blind.

Either way, Voussoir was immersed in seamless black ink, and she breathed again, out of surprise. And that was when the man's voice came for her, beginning with a name.

"Liza," he said.

Which happened to be the Master's rarely used birth name.

Then the man broke into loud laughter. The tone might have been joyous, might have been teasing. Either way, the cackling soon trailed away into a rough snort, and then the voice returned.

"Oh, it must be such a pleasure, Liza," he said. "You at last enjoying the honor of meeting me . . . "

7

"My name is Voussoir."

The words were spoken, but only as thought. Only in that remote portion of the mind where people are free and true. The rest of her considerable focus was shuffling instructions and the Master's biography as well as her native pissed-off sensibilities. Then the borrowed mouth repeated one critical word.

"'Honor.'"

No reaction.

"Who am I honored to meet?"

Silence.

"Share your name," she insisted.

"Oh and I would, if I had any to surrender," the voice replied. "But my attitude is that names are useless. Nothing but arbitrary noise flung against indifferent baryons and energy."

"My baryons are interested," she said.

His response was a soft, mocking laugh.

"Screw you," she thought, in secret.

The voice came closer, became louder.

"Consider the galaxy," he said. "A mighty whirlpool of dust and suns, and it wants no name. It needs nothing of the kind. Yet millions of living worlds hang labels upon this magnificence. Gifts of diction and history and hubris. And be honest now, Liza. Please. Can you genuinely believe that your Earth, the sphere on which you were conceived, understands what you intend when you point to the sky, talking fondly about a Milky Way?"

She gave him a hard laugh. "I'm standing with a philosopher," she said. "Fair warning, I have little patience for your species."

"I agree," he said. "You do rather despise intellectuals."

Voussoir offered her own stubborn silence.

"So let's dance with less obtuse concepts," he continued. "Gravity. Magnetism. Metabolic fire, and the fierce press of time. Unlike fanciful names, these are hard principles. These are features not only shared by every portion of the galaxy, but also help define the universe we see today and saw yesterday too."

"Who the hell are you?" she asked.

Laughter exploded—a cackle both charming, and in the same moment, unnerving.

Voussoir tried to step away. Except her new feet were swollen fiftyfold, or she was rooted directly into the granite. Or maybe the nerves between wishes and motion had been severed.

"Time," said the nameless companion. "Thoughtful life often holds to one broadly popular model of time. Though there are exceptions, and maybe we should list them. Just to prove how well-informed we are."

"No thank you," she said.

"Perhaps later," he said.

Then, "Standard counts of time place *Homo sapiens* among the exceptionally young. Not half a million Earth-years ago. That's when your faces and hands emerged. What's more, half your history was spent squatting beside dirty fires, eating feral meats, carving animal teeth, happily sharing tales about all manner of tiny subjects. Then, as often happens with busy hands, the stone and ivory gave way to iron and diamond, and your conversations became more expansive, more durable. And after only a few millennia, you transformed your cradle world. Tritium bombs and those early spacecraft were ready to save humanity, or destroy you. Look at your history honestly. Look at your life, Liza. There had to be one day when both those grand possibilities were equally eager to come true. And how would that story have ended . . . you don't know. You can never know. Because there was another day when one of your orbiting telescopes happened to see a rich flash of laser light. An alien beacon was enjoying an intense conversation with a very distant mate, in a language built to be understood, and on that momentous afternoon, a nameless ball of metal rock water and oxygen—the place where you happened to live—passed through the beacon. Purely by chance. And that's when humanity found herself suddenly holding the tools for ageless life, for starships, and for world-scale terraforming.

"All at once, the universe lay in your reach."

A pause arrived, lingered.

"I remember," Voussoir lied. "I was there."

"But where could you travel inside those fine new starships, those sturdy ageless bodies? Older, more capable aliens had already given the galaxy better names than your lactation nonsense. Every rich easy world knew the faces and hands of other creatures. What's more, broad customs and some stubbornly inflexible galactic laws kept your treachery to a minimum. Humans had little choice but make the best of sunless worlds, ill-suited moons, and solar systems on the fringes of what is normally regarded as respectable space."

Offended, Voussoir muttered, "'The vigorous limp makes the other leg strong.'"

"Ah, a harum-scarum proverb." The voice retreated slightly. "Yes, let's pay tribute to that ancient, prosperous species. Harum-scarums were exactly that. Early to the stars. Aggressive, risk-embracing natures, but with a survivor's laudable skill to know when to slink away. The Clan of the Many Clans has wandered across much of the galaxy, including some intriguing visits to your cradle. What passes for their empire is stable and happily rich, making both of their legs feel strong. Perhaps that success was why they maintained only a cursory watch over the deep dark beyond the galaxy.

"Crippled little humanity didn't have that luxury.

"And now, a second telescope demands mention. Drifting in the intergalactic cold, a human-built array of mirrors was tasked with finding incoming objects. The vast majority were natural, and that included some very substantial bolides. Sunless worlds often get flung out of galaxies. Asymmetric supernova and well-placed neutron stars do the same. After all, this is a universe built on compelling forces, and that means the occasional Uranus-class mass being accelerated to one-third light speed.

"Your telescope found such an object. Bigger and much faster than most, yes. But with cosmic dust and cometary ice laid over the hyperfiber hull, the invader didn't appear special. Truth demanded a better look, and that's why the nearest humans built and launched a tiny probe, kicking it to near-light velocities, and that's why it was the probe's resident AI who had the honor of peering behind the leading face, discovering a forest of giant rocket cones looming over a hull already billions of years old.

"The ultimate derelict. That was the Great Ship. No traces of crew, no legal mark of ownership, and according to the galaxy's ancient laws, ready to be owned by whoever stood first on its hull.

"And that's how one infantile chimp—a beast with little history and an uncommon amount of luck—won the universe's most wondrous prize."

8

Again, Voussoir tried to move.

But not with the legs. She had given up on those limbs. This time it was the right arm and its meaty hand, and against expectations, both of them easily lifted up, the Master's fingers clumsily sweeping through the blackness, feeling nothing. But the voice had come from a rather different direction, and like a navigator with only one point to steer by, Voussoir stabbed at a mouth that could only be imagined.

Her reach was met with heat and damp breath, and then pain, bright swift and done, leaving two fingertips suddenly stolen away.

Startled, embarrassed, then nothing but furious, Voussoir pulled back the hand, contemplating violence and violent words before falling back on safer tactics.

"'The universe's most wondrous prize,'" she quoted. "Is that what the Great Ship is?"

"As true as any statement ever made," the voice replied. "Inarguable and safe from fools."

A stranger's hand, human in feel and size, took hold of the wounded fingers, then an irresistible power pulled them away from her body while a second hand caressed the forearm. Then the severed fingertips were returned, set on top of the clotted blood, both beginning to splice themselves back into familiar flesh.

Anger fell into an equally useless gratitude.

Voussoir attempted to regain the conversation. "Your babble-pocket promised news about my ship."

"That's the impression I hoped to give, yes."

"And a looming danger."

"That the Master should hear about, yes."

She took a breath, holding it deep.

"Yes, Liza?"

"The old language you used . . . "

"Not old at all. Except in human terms."

"Why Khoisan?"

"You assume I have reasons. Instructive, illuminating reasons. And insights might spring from this personal information."

"You're very old," she said.

"Is that what you guess?"

"But I don't know which species you are."

"A word I work to avoid . . . "

"'Species?'"

"Live long enough, my dear, and you become a species of one."

She said nothing.

He matched her silence.

"You're at least as old as humanity," she finally said. "But I'm not impressed. I've met a few passengers who claim to have been born before the mammalian line."

"Most are lying to you," the voice said.

"Presumably."

"Do you wish to know who tells the truth?"

"Yes."

"No, I don't believe you." The tone was sharp, words delivered by a mouth that had suddenly circled behind her. "I will admit this much: I carry an extraordinary amount of time. Massively ancient, I was, when I first arrived on your homeworld. And there you were, Liza . . . squatting by the fire, telling fables to one another."

"You're harum-scarum," she said.

He laughed again, seemingly roaring his approval, and all the while she heard the mouth working, the jaws hard and sharp. A mock-bird's beak, or maybe a giant insect's mandibles. Voussoir imagined her neck bitten, the entire head sliced from these shoulders. Two decapitations in one day . . . and that's why she straightened her back, ready to endure the insult.

Something about the situation amused her companion.

Then his chuckling faded away.

She was alone.

For an hour, perhaps. Voussoir tried to count moments, count breaths, but her internal clock was peculiarly confused. The silence might have been much longer than an hour, or nothing passed but the illusion of breath and numbers, heartbeats and the swing of a pendulum.

When the voice returned, it began by quietly saying, "Apologies, Liza. I was needed elsewhere."

"Doing what?" she asked.

She expected no answers.

But what felt very much like a human mouth was pressed near an ear, and a whisper both slow and quite loud said, "You know what it is to rule, Liza. The demands never end."

"And what do you rule?" she asked.

"One small maelstrom of stars," he said. "Named for a fluid that has never flowed from your breasts. That's what I hold in my grip. Or at least some significant portion of that wonder."

"You rule the galaxy," she said.

And she made a point of laughing at him.

He answered with a put-upon snort. Nothing more.

She let a bold mood take hold, saying, "It's such an honor to meet you, my Lord Gravity. A wondrous force such as yourself, given this voice and made tiny enough to stand beside spellbound me."

She said, "Truly, the Master Captain has never enjoyed a greater honor."

At which point, he touched her face.

A long and frigid claw was slowly dragged across the lips.

"What is your name, little girl?"

The question came from no mouth. Welling up from her blood, those irresistible words demanded an answer, and the same blood surrendered.

"Voussoir," she said.

"That I did not know," he said in turn.

Then he laughed with patience and warmth, adding, "Perhaps you don't realize how much of joy it is, Voussoir . . . these endless moments when the universe reminds me that I understand only a little more than what all of you can ever know."

9

"Soldiers are currency, and every captain keeps us inside a favorite purse."

That was one version of the barracks maxim. G heard the words after putting on the recruits' gray uniform, and repeating them with enthusiasm proved his place in the ranks. But embracing the cynicism came later, after graduation and a few centuries of competent service, and particularly after his first genuine war. Several dozen colleagues died during the fights, which might not make an impressive stack of bodies. But that was forty-nine millennia ago, and if all of those men and women had survived—if they were standing inside the bunker today, lined up beside the former Lieutenant G—they would be carrying more years of happy life than all the troops who ever marched into any of the famous old wars.

Every good soldier needed to be scared of death, but G had a rare capacity to ignore nonexistence, focusing only on his immediate work. That certainly helped explain his persistent rise through an organization that lost few bodies in the average decade. Becoming the Ship's Marshall was one ambition fulfilled, and he intended to hold this office until scandals in the ranks or a tragedy in battle forced the Master Captain to find her scapegoat. And then, because he was a good soldier, G would resign in some public manner, convincing passengers and crew alike that She was in charge and She had zero patience for any shade of incompetence.

And then?

Retirement, perhaps. Though G often dreamed about little posts and low profiles, ignored by the captains through the next fifty scandals. That's how you survived in this realm. Wait and wait, and eventually the Master would need another new Marshall, and their G would be a reliable agent ruling some sleepy district. That's how he would rise again, eventually finding himself standing inside another hardened bunker, shoulder to shoulder with hundreds and thousands of ghost soldiers, while Miocene stood before him, in all her glacial majesty.

G watched the First Chair with his living eye while its mechanical partner absorbed torrents of data and virtual videos. The nearby chamber had proved as unremarkable as everyone hoped it would be. No entity or sentient device had appeared inside it, and nothing within a hundred kilometers acted even remotely interested in what was happening here. Playing her part in the game, Voussoir stood in the middle of that stone chamber, crossing time until she was free to turn and leave again. Then the moment arrived, and the soldier attempted to leave, but the little lamp was turned off or it failed, or perhaps it was stolen away, and that's when the Vermiculate suddenly reclaimed its night.

"Well," seemed like too little to say. But that's exactly what Miocene offered, with a tight quiet voice.

"Shit," was the Marshall's addition to that potent dialogue.

No sound emerged from the chamber. Not breathing or curses or even the steady thrumming of one ageless heart. Sensors continued to peer inside the stone cubbyhole, and maybe Voussoir was there. Or maybe not. Neither of G's eyes were sure what they were witnessing. The only authority full of confidence was one AI savant designed for this single contingency.

"I still see the Master's body," the machine stated.

Its tone was intrigued, excited. Giddy.

"And I see someone invading the body, subverting nexuses and resident safeguards."

A primary fear, always.

"Failure is imminent," it warned.

Which was when Miocene, the ultimate survivor, did as she had done so many times in the past.

With a glance, she told her Marshall, "The responsibility is yours."

G opened a shielded nexus while burying his natural sympathies, and then he gave seven camouflaged blinds permission to unholster their weapons, then fire.

10

For some soldiers, wounds were a reliable delight. Severed limbs, shattered faces, intestines dangling pink and slick outside the eviscerated body cavity. Insults like that became a warrior's drama that deserved to be told again and again. With drink and with lovers. Or when alone, entirely sober. Battlefield mayhem needed to be described in detail, including your own calm mind and the rapid, equally violent healing process. The grateful leg was always shoved back into its socket, arteries and nerves rebuilt in minutes. New eyes emerged from the gore, along with a mouth spitting the worst alien curses. And what to do with the dangling guts? Folding them back inside the body took too long, which was why field blades sliced and hands tugged, the intestines abandoned so that the fight could press on.

But Voussoir despised being wounded. Injuries were embarrassments that proved sloppy work, and worse, sour luck. No matter how tough the body or how quickly flesh and skeletons regrew, injuries always surprised Voussoir. Like the night when a fat uranium slug punched through her chest, removing the heart and a long piece of spine. That disaster came at the end of the battle, and because the bioceramic brain was practically infinite, Voussoir could recall every detail: the feel of the ground beneath her ass; the stink of ozone and enemy pheromones; sirens telling the F"foon civilians to remain in their burrows; and how her entire squad filed past their lieutenant's helpless body, shoving a few fingers inside the gaping hole while sharing the usual rough-natured insults.

Voussoir was being wounded now.

Worse than ever before, she realized.

"The fingertips you gave me," she began.

"Yes?"

"Aren't mine."

"But they are the same fingers, Voussoir. Augmented to help with their critical work."

"You're attacking my nexuses."

"Machines that don't belong to you either, do they?"

A tentacle or animated rope claimed the Master's wrist, locking it in place, while a furnace surrounded the hand, cooking its flesh.

She said, "I'm not the Master Captain."

"On that, we agree."

"Buffers. Isolators. Embedded mandates."

"Safeguards protecting the nexuses and shielding the Great Ship too. Yes, these precautions are doing their heroic work."

Fire shot through the forearm, finding her chest.

Voussoir tried to collapse but couldn't. Except then the granite floor rose up, slamming against her back.

She gasped, retrieving a breath or two.

"You promised to tell," she said.

From the darkness above, her torturer replied with a hard click of the tongue.

She said, "The Great Ship is threatened . . . by you . . . ?"

"That's what you believe?"

"Yes."

"Then you are mistaken."

Flames leaped out of her and then returned as ice. Suddenly every tissue attached to her was transformed into a glassy solid. Yet Voussoir still had enough voice to beg. "Please," she said. "Tell me one true thing."

"Just one? Oh, very well."

What was bizarre only grew more so. Her captor carefully stretched out on the floor beside her, and what felt like a human arm was eased between stone and skull, giving her a pillow to rest against.

She imagined a powerful man's arm and matching body.

"Lord Gravity," he said.

Then, "In this universe, that particular god is inevitable."

Voussoir's frozen face couldn't move, much less speak. Yet the Master's voice rose out of her, asking, "What the hell are you saying?"

"Gravity is fundamental to nature," he said. "Electromagnetism and quantum mechanics too. A weave-work of relationships involves mathematics, energy, and particles, each relationship emerging at the beginning of the beginning, or shortly thereafter."

"Granted," she managed.

"But much else is inevitable. Life, for example. And in countless places, there is intelligent, self-aware thought."

Staring into the ink, Voussoir considered too many questions.

"Now answer this," he continued. "When did intelligence first emerge from the young Creation?"

School-learned dates offered their advice.

Voussoir shared a few numbers.

"Whose civilization was first?"

Candidates lined up for her, and she said, "The Bakers."

"Why them?"

"I like their name," she admitted. "When I was little, they fascinated me."

"Why?"

"Because they built incredible machines. The best machines ever, maybe. Dead for several billion years, but the galaxy is littered with their creations, many of them still capable and eager to work."

With that, a lovely whistle fell from everywhere. Then the mouth beside her explained, "Of course they never referred to themselves as 'Bakers.' That's just an inadequate translation shoved through human expectations. Yet as ancient as the Bakers were, they were far from the first creatures to stand in sunlight, admiring their own short shadows."

"Who was first?" she asked.

No answer.

"You?"

Laughter rolled over her, warm again, and soothing.

Voussoir enjoyed that sound far too much.

"Let me share this much, my friend. No portion of your sky is special. Every nameless whirlpool of dust and fusion produces an initial crop of life. Watery organics. Wise crystals. Structured plasmas found nowhere but on the edges of newborn black holes. The specific path to consciousness and civilization hardly matters. Results are always the same. The First emerge from every newborn galaxy, and that includes the trillions of galaxies beyond the edge of the visible universe. Gravity reigns and so do they, spreading fast, and after a few aeons, those fortunate creatures will have answered every question worth asking.

"As fundamental as protons," he said. "Every First Generation is that."

He paused.

"So where are they today?" she asked.

"Lying down beside you in the dark, obviously."

Another pause arrived, and it felt long.

Though it wasn't.

Voussoir gathered up more questions. But as soon as she spoke, the voice cut her off.

"Oh, I am prepared to tell you everything," he promised. "But a problem has emerged. Your superior officer is attempting to cripple me or murder me. Which is quite unfortunate since you are the only one in danger, and that leaves you with an exceptionally difficult choice, Voussoir.

"Hear the truth about everything, but die.

"Or we stop now, inside this moment, and I save you as you are . . . a beautiful soul wandering through this frail universe of mine . . . "

11

Seven whisks of antimatter iron rode inside magnetic fields, each wrapped within hair-thin jackets of hyperfiber and iridium, and at nearly two percent light speed, those jackets were spat down seven holes that had been carved by X-ray lasers and some exceptionally delicate harmonics.

Monuments to cleverness and calculation, the weapons were also burdened with rich opportunities for error.

Sister-Witch was standing tall on her piece of granite, defending the tunnel and the Master Captain, and if possible, protecting her own life too. Field sensors had consistently reported what she expected to see, which was nothing. For more than twelve hundred seconds, the Master had stood just out of reach of eyeballs, partly filling the most insignificant room in the universe. "Thank the spirits that Voussoir watches over us," she kept thinking. Then the Master's lamp was extinguished. Sister-Witch knew nothing about any attack on the nexuses or the Marshall's violent response. Yet if she had known, nothing would have changed. Her stance was comfortable, but not too comfortable. That's how she kept herself alert and ready. Her only failure was not being able to fend off the imaginary foes. Bioceramic brains had too much capacity, and few soldiers were as creative as Sister-Witch, and that's why a broad slice of her mind was dedicated to a pretend battle between her rail gun and the furious beast charging from behind, razored scales and one gaping mouth facing for her.

Seven distant weapons fired one round each.

Three cartridges reached their target, intersecting at a point just above the chamber and the helpless body.

Three more rounds detonated early, while the fourth somehow managed to arrive nanoseconds late, and deflected by one miniscule thermonuclear event, it was flung straight up the tunnel where Sister-Witch was standing.

She didn't feel the impact, didn't register the exceptionally narrow wound or its subsequent healing. That cartridge continued on its way, detonating a few hundred meters farther along, and while native rock absorbed the blast, the bunker's floor shook hard enough to make every eye open a little wider than before.

The united three-cartridge blast was larger and much closer to Sister-Witch, and since every explosion is lazy, the plasma bloom tried to flow through the only available exit. Sensors screamed with a data-rich panic, and she saw the flash, and then she was on her ass, a minor diagnostic tool warning her that her hyperfiber armor was pierced through the chest and the back, and how did she feel?

Pissed.

Alive.

Fucking glorious.

Then she was standing again. An atmosphere of oxygen and gloom had been replaced with atomized rock and a nearly perfect silence. Designed for fighting in alien environments, her helmet built a faceplate that sealed tight, then fed her chest cold bottled oxygen. But breathing was only a habit at this point. Someone was trying to murder the Master Captain, and existence had no purpose but to push ahead, testing armors and life-support systems until they failed, then discovering that she was still a few steps short of her goal.

The Master Captain lay on the soft floor, the uniform incinerated along with most of the body inside. What remained was an enormous silhouette of soot driven into the flowing stone, arms held at their sides as if utterly relaxed, the one-time head waiting at Sister-Witch's feet.

Nexuses and voices were shouting.

Commands, overlapping and obvious.

She shut all of them down and raised her rail gun. Dislodging the bioceramic brain took moments and too much time, but at least the Master was cradled in her arms, and turning, the would-be savior attempted to escape the room on feet that were beginning to burn.

Lava fell from the ceiling, striking her shoulder.

The pain was set aside.

Then it began to rain molten rock. Her armor was breached, her body was burning, and she ran on her ragged knees until she fell over. Then, on the premise that the rest of the squad was waiting inside the tunnel, she tried tossing the mind to them. But her arms were useless too, what with the muscle gone and the blood turned to steam. It was all that Sister-Witch could manage, curling up around the Master Captain, protecting her with those final kilograms of skeleton and hyperfiber.

This inferno was so much worse than any monster she had imagined.

That was Sister-Witch's final thought before Death took hold, then set about deciding what to do with her next.

12

Gray twilight ruled the hallway and presumably every room beyond. Facing her many guests, the apartment's sole tenant greeted them with a wave of the hand and the words, "Come. Be with me. Everyone." Then with majestic grace, that newly conjured body turned and quickly strode away.

"Of course, madam," said Miocene, following the Master Captain through the gloom.

Marshall G was last inside. Overlapping doorways sealed while the resident surveillance system spoke only to him. "Wait, sir. Wait." Electric fingers began to massage his frame, and with nowhere to go, G considered how more sensitive individuals might take offense. After all, the heightened alerts had been allowed to expire. And he should know, being the Head of Security and all.

"Thank you so much, sir," the system offered. "You may go wherever you wish."

Even by Ship standards, the Master's apartment was extravagant: One cubic kilometer filled with thousands of rooms, many of them defined by towering walls, arched ceilings, and a hectare of floor, or more. Every room was littered with ornate furnishings and the rarest artwork, diamond biospheres filled with exotic life, plus baubles and quirky marvels—one-of-a-kinds given by all manner of grateful passengers. Yet very few rooms were used on a regular basis, and some may never have been seen by the Master Captain. Famously immune to snobbery, she craved familiar food and familiar comfort. Standing anywhere, armed with nexuses and habit, she was also everywhere else inside a singular starship, and how could a thousand pretty paintings compete against that?

The Master led her guests to a modest parlor. Marshall G had been in this room many times before. A living couch always stood near the doorway, waiting to serve. Woven from three unrelated beasts of burden, none of them sentient, the organism had three pampered mouths and one shared anus, fur and fat and firm muscle creating a platform just smart enough to always make itself comfortable for its owner.

The Master Captain reached the couch and spun about. But then the knees locked. She didn't sit.

As if startled, the couch twitched.

No one spoke, not with mouths or nexuses. The Master had just today recovered her bulk, her nexuses replaced and rapidly returning to work. In that dim light, she towered over her audience. Every face appeared simple and every sound felt enlarged, vivid and close. A dozen Submasters were present, Miocene standing in front of her subordinates. The guest of honor stood closest to Marshall G, but not close enough to touch. Her body was a full day younger than the Master's body, making it newborn. Cultured from the resident genetics, unfinished legs shook whenever they did too much work, and standing seemed especially taxing at the moment.

"You should sit," was the Master's advice.

"Thank you, madam," said Voussoir, and ignoring various chairs, she dropped to the harum-scarum rug that covered the local floor. And again, the soldier said, "Thank you, madam."

The Master glanced at her First Chair.

Miocene was ready to wait forever, feigning patience.

But there was no need. "I have a confession to share," said the Master.

"And that would be?"

"I just discovered an unexpected, wondrous joy."

With that news, Miocene nodded, eyebrows raised.

A broad hand was lifted high, and that captains' captain swept it back and forth before her round face. "The most intense pleasure that I have ever known."

Marshall G saw a duty to fill. "How intriguing, madam."

The Master glanced at him, halfway smiling. "You see, my hands lost their grip on the helm. I felt like a youngster again, without talent, without responsibility. For several hours, I had nothing to occupy my sanity but small thoughts about my very few needs."

"And that's what made you happy," G began.

"Oh, goodness, no." The hard laugh signaled disgust, disappointment. Perhaps the Master would dress G down now, as a warning. But she couldn't shake what had made her so happy, and as she smiled again, hands closing into fists, the First Chair answered for her.

"When you took back the helm," said Miocene.

"Exactly," the Master Captain said. "I have always assumed that I knew what ecstasy is. But obviously I didn't. Not until I took back the Great Ship, I didn't."

A brief silence was allowed.

Then the Great Ship's ruler turned to the fellow who presently served as the Marshall. "So what have we learned today, G? Tell me."

One thousand centuries wasn't enough time to populate more than a sliver of the Great Ship. The interior was still jammed of wilderness, unlit and uninhabited, and only mapping savants could count the places that had never been modified by busy tools. Most of the Vermiculate fell into that category. But not the one room where Voussoir had gone. Nanological tools had converged on that tiny space, and setting to work, they moved every silicon and oxygen aside before slathering the gaps with all manner of camouflage. Then the original atoms were set back in place. That's how the trap had been built. Atom by atom, over quite a few careful centuries, the conspirator had presumably done little else, and except for a few tweaks from rare and expensive technologies, nothing about the project was amazing.

"What impresses is the commitment of time and intricacy," Marshall G offered. "As much as ten thousand years chasing this one narrow venture."

The Master already knew the verdict, but it was important to hear the synopsis aloud, absorbing the lessons in a public way. A major portion of her job was stagecraft, and she knew how to wear a concerned face, knew how many times to nod, and recognizing the perfect moment, she subsequently turned to her First Chair, calmly asking, "And what about our enemy?"

Another mystery resolved.

Miocene shared what might be the most complete study ever made of a blast site. Megawatts were on display, radioactive tracks radiating out through stone, and under the magma rain, the Master's former body: charred tissue and bone shards punctuated with a few hundred nexuses as big as pepper grains, and thousands more that were exponentially smaller. Not one of those critical machines had survived the blast—as planned, yes, and thank goodness. An eddy inside the flowing plasma was what saved Voussoir's brain, and then Sister-Witch chiseled her free and carried her just far enough to save both of them from the searing heat.

At that point, Voussoir interrupted Miocene.

"How is she?"

The First Chair's gaze remained fixed on the Master Captain. "She might be healthier than you, as it happens. But we don't need to hurry her recovery. So the surgeons are taking their time."

"Of course, madam. Thank you."

Only Marshall G watched his soldier. By logic or chance, the newest body resembled a half-finished adolescent, very tall but slight, thin legs crossed, ankles and long feet resting against the silver and blue harum-scarum rug.

Voussoir's face was pointed downward, fingers playing with the glass weave.

Miocene continued. "This is the attacker. Here."

Two of the Master's fingers had been removed, replaced by what looked like an interrogation device, but was really much more. Ages ago, a species of AIs known as Brink Riders had boarded the Great Ship, traveling from their supercooled homeland to another sunless Pluto-class body. All but one had disembarked at the proper point and time. Remaining behind, in secret, the tiny stowaway busied itself by refashioning a portion of the Vermiculate, and when the opportunity arrived, it contrived a way to grab hold of the Master's hand.

"And it might have won," Miocene allowed. "If winning meant gaining control of the Ship and every major system onboard, then yes, there was a real danger. If we had allowed you to stroll into the trap, only routine security in place, there would have been a one-in-eleven-hundred chance of success. Which to a Brink Rider is an exceptionally enticing promise."

"But with precautions in place . . . " G began to ask.

"One chance in an ocean of failure," was how Miocene settled the matter. "But again, Brink Riders have a courage that humans rarely understand."

Small dangers or not, the attacker had been killed.

Marshall G absorbed that verdict while staring at his soldier, trying to read expressions on a face that was always a little new.

The Master Captain said, "Voussoir."

Up went the eyes, then back down again. "Yes, madam."

"Your name. It's rather popular with the Family. Am I right?"

"Yes, madam."

"It means—?"

"'The wedge that holds high the arch,'" she replied.

"Interesting," the Master offered. Such a perfect word that it needed to be said twice again. "Interesting, interesting."

Voussoir's eyes were closed tight, skeletal fingers moving faster through the harum-scarum weave.

"Your report, Voussoir. It's detailed, very thorough. But tell it to me now, as if I know nothing."

The fingers grew still.

"Voussoir?"

Eyes lifted, and it seemed as if all of the face opened wide. "I walked to where I was ordered to walk, stood where I was supposed to stand, waited the proper time, then turned to leave again."

"And?"

"Nothing."

The lords of the Great Ship stared at the soldier who was folded up and sitting at their feet.

Again, Voussoir said, "Nothing."

Then before more questions were asked, she added, "Oh, I've tried to remember. I do want to help you. But except for sharp teeth biting off the fingers, I have nothing to offer you . . . "

13

Eventually there was a morning when Voussoir woke up to find the same powerful build and identical blonde curls that he had worn a little more than a century ago. Yes, the hands were smaller than they had been, and the genitals sported their own structural quirks. But there were too many similarities to count, and even though Voussoir didn't want to believe in signs, a portion of him had no choice but to think, "Today has to be the day."

His spouse woke up female, and they shared the bed for a little while before she decided, "You're distracted."

"Rather so," he admitted.

"Is something wrong?"

"Somewhere, yes. But not here." Then he focused on the work until both were happy, and while clothes adjusted to their new frames, Voussoir mentioned that he had to leave on an errand.

She eyed him and then looked elsewhere.

"All right then," she said.

Three decades of marriage, with considerable talk of making a child. But each of them still kept secrets, and they had never agreed about whether or not to raise the progeny in the Family of Perpetual Renewal. Both of them held strong opinions on this critical matter, and as often happens with functional immortals, both were prepared to wait another thousand years to win the argument.

Alone, Voussoir left the little apartment, walking to the nearest public cap-car, and after a short ride to an adjacent district, he took a second, much quicker car, paying the premium to obscure his route and destination. Yet even then, he ran the final kilometers, and that's why it was late in the day when he reached an enclave that had been declared Forbidden by the Master herself.

Two black-garbed soldiers recognized something in Voussoir's face or gait. One nodded warily, and the other asked, "Off duty?"

"Retired," he said. "Sixty years, nearly."

"You like civilian life?" she asked.

"Only when I'm not being shot," he said.

They shared a good laugh, then the wary soldier mentioned that it was time for one of them to walk on.

"G," Voussoir said.

They stared at him.

"Tell him that I'm here."

"And who are you?"

Voussoir offered his name and former rank.

"The Admiral's awfully busy with his little war," the woman warned. But barely ten seconds passed before orders arrived, and not only was the retired soldier given full access, but the suspicious guard was told to bring the honored guest directly to the command bunker.

"Who are you?" both soldiers asked again.

But Voussoir had already told them as much as he was comfortable with, and that was why he refused to offer any more words, including, "Thank you."

Only the two men stood inside the bunker. On the walls, shifting portals gazed out across a heavily urbanized district. Local humans were on the march, hordes of them, competing banners held high, kinetic weapons in every hand's reach. This city was ruled by cults and old grievances. This was an Archaic community, meaning that the residents were human but not immortal. A realm of soft tissue souls, brains wet and temporary, this was very much like a tiny slice of Old Earth. Voussoir was fascinated with what he saw, what he heard, and in particular, one barely adult man who lay dead in the middle of a crossroads. A lead bullet had punched two holes in his skull, one hole tiny and the other quite huge, and Voussoir was wondering if the corpse was being left as a message or a warning. Or maybe the boy had been forgotten for the time being. Which would be the worst possible circumstance, and maybe someone who could ignore bullets would walk down there and take care of this little problem.

G watched his companion for some patient while. Then he made a reasonable guess. "You managed to remember something. Didn't you?"

"Oh, I never forgot any of it," Voussoir confessed.

The two of them traded glances, careful smiles. Then the former Marshall said, "I had a feeling. When you sat on the Master's floor like you did . . . I assumed you were pissed about being used as bait and nearly killed."

"Except I would have taken that trade," said Voussoir. "My life in order to save the Great Ship, and helping kill an enemy in the process . . . "

"Is that what happened? Did we execute the attacker?"

"I'd like to think so."

G said nothing.

"This is what I remember," Voussoir said. Then after one deep breath, he spoke with precision, reproducing every word and the exact pauses between, ending after he reached the moment when the stranger's voice said, "Or we stop now, inside this moment, and I save you as you are . . . a beautiful soul wandering through this frail universe of mine . . . "

With one silent command, G closed down the portals, and with a quiet word, he filled the bunker with the yellow-white light of Sol, midday and brilliant. Then he sat on the hard floor, legs crossed, and Voussoir did the same, facing him, close enough that it wasn't much of a reach for them to hold hands.

For one man, an hour of hard concentration brought up many possibilities. But the other man had a century of reflection to offer up. Yes, the AI mastermind might be dead, and the First Civilization and humanity's guided luck were nothing but noise flung against gullible baryons and energy. But what if the story was true? What if ancient entities knew every important answer but were now hiding out of sight? And if all that was so, what careful next step might be worth the expense and the risks?

G mentioned the obvious duty: approach Miocene or even the Master Captain. "I could certainly earn their attention, if I wanted that."

"But I don't want that," Voussoir said.

"So. You're afraid they belong to the First."

"Oh, no. Never." Feeling a little sickened by the suggestion, Voussoir spent a moment shaking his head and wiping his mouth hard. With the day getting long, he contemplated a little dose of sleep, reasoning that changing his voice might make him sound a little less paranoid.

"Why don't you want to warn them?" G persisted.

"Because," Voussoir began.

Then he hesitated. This was so much harder than he had imagined . . .

G's living eye grew larger, brighter. "Wait. You stopped telling the story, but the story didn't stop. Did it?"

A slow nod. Then, "'This frail universe of mine,' he said. Which was when I told him, 'I'm not all that frail, and we'll probably never talk again. So go on. Share a little more, and maybe I'll get out here just fine.'

"Very well,' he said.

"He said, 'They are coming.'

"'They? You mean the First Generation.'

"'To take what they want.'

"'The Great Ship,' I said.

"They'll take it for reasons. Honorable reasons and very selfish reasons, and every cause in between.'

"'But you're already here,' I pointed out.

"'Except I don't want them to take the Ship.'

"'You want it for yourself,' I said.

"'For honorable and selfish reasons, I do.'

"'That is interesting to hear.'

"Then his voice got faster, and he told me, 'Make ready. When they come for you, and they will come for you soon, you must be ready.'"

Voussoir paused.

G shifted his rump against the hard floor.

"That's when your three bullets came for me," Voussoir said. "And I heard nothing else. Not the voice, and not the explosion."

"I gave the order to fire," G said.

"I know."

"Maybe I'm one of the First."

"Actually, I'm rather hoping you are. Someone who knows something, hiding among us while wearing the perfect disguise."

"Shit, I wish I was someone else. About every day, I do. But as far as I can tell, I'm nothing but another ex-Marshall struggling with an endless and thankless shit assignment."

Voussoir shrugged. "Well, I knew that was too much to hope for."

G waited a long moment, then recrossed old ground. "And you don't want to tell this story to the Master."

He shook his head.

"Because the voice in the dark might be our friend . . . ?"

"Ally or enemy, it doesn't matter." Voussoir retrieved his hands, drying them against his trouser legs. "The more I think about his talents, his genius . . . and even if only half of what he said is halfway true . . . believing that the captains could ever fool someone like him becomes more and more ludicrous. Which means that he must have known what sort of stooge would be sent to meet him, and the whole extraordinary show was intended for one lieutenant standing deep in the ranks."

G nodded slowly, then said, "So you didn't come here to confess. A hundred years to make ready, and I imagine—tell me if I'm wrong—I can see you bringing along a battle plan or two."

"Of course," Voussoir said.

"And the plan is?"

The man who once wore the Master's body and then spoke to a god had to summon up the energy to stand. Then with a shrug of the broad shoulders, he said, "As a high-ranking officer serving the most powerful military machine in the known universe . . . sir, I assume you have a few tools and leftover powers that you might want to share for a good cause . . . "

14

Thousands of years passed, and all that time, the interrogation chamber remained black and empty. Empty and invisible. Those who had so carefully fabricated it were elsewhere. Some died when the Troubles came, and quite a few more were lost after the Great Ship was stolen. But enough had survived in the shadows, and more good souls were brought into the secret works, leading to the moment when all that perfect darkness suddenly came to an end.

A simple light no brighter than a weakly burning candle took life.

From the darkness on one side, a woman's voice said, "All right now. Come close."

The old soldier stepped into the glow, dragging the manacled prisoner by one of its jointed limbs.

"Sister-Witch," said the woman's voice.

Sister-Witch made certain that she trusted her grip. Then she reached out, ready for any hand that came out to meet hers.

ABOUT THE AUTHOR

Robert Reed is the author of nearly three hundred published stories, plus more than a dozen novels. He is best known for his Great Ship stories, including The Memory of Sky. And for the novella, "A Billion Eves," which won the Hugo Award in 2007. He lives in Lincoln, Nebraska with his wife and daughter.

No Way Back

CHI HUI TRANSLATED BY JOHN CHU

Master Hacker

11:30 a.m.

knock, knock, knock.

"Hey, Xuejiao, someone's knocking at the door." Aksha puts its paw on my face.

"I know." I roll over to my other side, pull the blanket over my head, and continue to dream happy dreams.

knock, knock, knock.

Aksha burrows out from under the blanket, stretches gracefully, and nudges away a few pellets of last night's cat food. Distastefully, it lies prone next to my pillow: "There. Is. Some. One. At. The. Door. Xia. Xue. Jiao."

"I fucking know!" I get up, throwing off the blanket.

Carelessly, I kick over the half box of instant noodles I put next to the bed three days ago. They scatter all over the place. The room was never large, but now it looks especially small and narrow.

knock, knock, knock.

I put on some clothes I grab at random and trample through paper and dirty laundry to get to the door. Through the peephole, I see a middle-aged man standing in front of the door. His face is numb, holding no particular expression. He's braced as though he will knock down the door if I don't open it.

"Who do you want?" I shout grumpily through the door.

"I'm looking for . . . " The man breaks off suddenly. He takes a piece of paper from his suit pocket and holds it to the peephole. On the paper is written two words: Master Hacker.

"There's a place that sells knives downstairs and to the left," I yell back.

The door still closed, I grab two bags of milk and a box of cat food. Aksha runs toward me, its tail high in the air. It stares at me, regards the milk with disdain and the cat food with interest. For a cat, this expression passes for a serious one.

"Looking for a Master Hacker?"

"We move out this afternoon," I whisper back.

It snorts twice discontentedly and snatches the box of cat food out of my hand with its mouth. Cats don't like to leave their territory. Our vagabond life means we invariably have to leave before Aksha has had its way with the female cats in the neighborhood.

"Which rat bastard gave away where we live?" it grumbles as it eats up milk-soaked cat food. I suck at a bag of milk and begin to throw clothes into a suitcase.

knock, knock, knock.

I glance through the peephole. The man is really stubborn. He clearly has no plans of ever leaving.

With a crash, I throw open the door. My hands on my waist, I stand in front of the man. "Are you fucking sick in the head?"

The man stares dumbfounded. Perhaps chalk-dusted teachers who wear Western-style suits and trousers aren't used to being treated like this. Or maybe he expected a cruel, steely-eyed man, his cynical mind jacked into the net rather than a young woman staring back with bloodshot eyes.

"I'm looking for . . . a Master Hacker," he says with a small voice.

The door across the hall opens a crack. The retired woman stares from behind with interest, her gaze shifting up and down.

"Something to hack with, my ass. If you want a kitchen knife you can use to kill yourself, they sell them in the market downstairs. I don't sell them here. Would you like a rope to hang yourself with? What mental hospital shut down and set you free to go to someone's home to buy a kitchen knife? What is wrong with you? For fuck's sake, scram! You annoy me."

I slam the door shut. Inside the room, stuff crashes to the floor. Out of the corner of my eye, I see, through the window, the man leave. He seems much older suddenly.

"Did you track down his cell phone?" I gesture at Aksha.

"13330573885." Aksha lashes its tail. "Cheng Liang, male, forty-eight years old, chemistry professor at G University. I've already recorded his home address and IP address."

I stuff clean clothes into the suitcase, the dirty clothes into a big plastic bag, and toss them both on the bed. The computer case opens in one swift flick. I take out a hard drive and hide it in a pocket. A terse note is left for the landlord explaining that I've moved out. By the time Aksha grudgingly leaps into the cat carrier, the taxi I called for is already waiting downstairs.

One suitcase, one cat carrier, one cat, and one hard drive, this is the sum total of what I'm taking from the "nest" I lived in for four months. Everything else I'm leaving for the landlord, who rarely ever shows up. He might be able to figure me out from this stuff, but he'll have no way to track me down. Because I'm about to leave for a new place, I'm about to start another phase of my life.

It's always like this. My life is split by a series of moves. Sometimes, I can even hear the sound of my life slowly rotting in these wrecked memories. My life is an abject mess, unbearably vile. A woman ought to have the serene happiness I absolutely do not have. Obviously, I don't have a husband.

Men aren't capable of being a companion to a woman like me. So I have a chatty cat, who grudgingly regards itself as a partner in my career as a "Master Hacker."

But it generally finds female cats way more attractive.

Abyss

Without a whole lot of effort, I find a safe cubbyhole in another city one hundred and eighty kilometers away. The ID I use is my fourth set: a half-hearted effort, it pins all its hopes on being a young woman with a postgraduate diploma. The age and appearance are dead-on.

After settling in, my first order of business is to unpack my fully tricked out computer and get on the net. The landlord doesn't live here, but his son, before he leaves, earnestly helps me load in and install the computer. His gaze never leaves my low-cut dress.

The landlord proudly boasts that his son is a good student. He's in ninth grade and can absolutely test into a good school.

My cat glances at the whiskers on the boy's face. They grow up so fast these days.

At 2:00 a.m. the next day, I link into an abyss.

The network has many layers. Some people are content to merely skim the surface, enjoying the virtual images and information electrical brain stimulation brings them. A long time ago, people enjoyed opening doors that were closed to them. As a result, they became known as hackers. Then the brain-network interface was invented. Some people discovered certain places didn't have doors, but no one had ever set foot there. Stale data, long-disappeared records piled up in forgotten corners to the point that they were considered long-deleted secrets.

We call this sort of place an abyss.

Lots of people are happy to work for the government as "spelunkers," depending on their piddling skills, to excavate data from ancient abysses and convert them into cash. If their luck is good, they can make a fortune. But not everyone is content to be a spelunker. Some people like more extreme methods of making money or more direct means of grabbing money from the government. We call ourselves "Master Hackers."

When I'm online, Aksha keeps me company. Anyone who says cats can't go online is an idiot. Twenty years ago, people said humanity couldn't go to Mars. Ten years ago, people solemnly swore that there was no way to connect a human mind to the network. Five years ago, people said that cats and dogs couldn't speak.

As the facts show, they are all idiots.

Although being at the representational layer is like being a stranded fish placed back into water, once I sink into an abyss, Aksha astutely stops. It doesn't like these huge, distant data spaces. Hanging out just outside, it guards me against government surveillance programs.

Lots of people do not know how to find the abysses of "Master Hackers." They stare at unused servers, idle computers, not realizing there's a kind of abyss that they keep brushing past.

The servers Master Hackers use are always busy, especially the massively multiplayer online game databases. We use every trick in the book to set up our own development spaces.

I enter the game data from *World of Stars*. Within a dense of fog of calculations, I find the cleverly camouflaged door. A password as obvious as if it were carved into my memory matches a long string of characters like flowing water. The door within the illusion opens easily.

I never put any essential programs on my hard drive. The programs a smart Master Hacker uses are all hidden in the recesses of the network. They serve as the strongest and nimblest extensions of one's mind, radiating like a spiderweb in all directions.

For the same reason: If someone seizes the data within a Master Hacker's database, that person also has the Master Hacker in the palm of their hand. To tell the truth, when that man held up the piece of paper with "Master Hacker" written on it, I practically pissed my pants.

The database bears the marks of a break in. Some are meticulously and ingeniously concealed but leave some inadvertent loose ends.

Others are blatant, but are neatly cut off from its source. No way to trace them. A blast of cold flits across my back. I shudder in spite of myself.

An abyss is a place filled with danger. No one gets this. Whoever you meet, or the person who spies on you, is a government spelunker or a Master Hacker or is a ghost hidden inside a vast database. Spelunkers and Master Hackers pass around a saying you need to understand: Some abysses absolutely must not be tested. Hiding there are vast existences beyond our comprehension. All the jackholes who go there are drawn into a vortex of data, forever gone. They leave behind stiff bodies, lying comatose in hospital ICUs.

"Have you found the bastard?" Aksha's consciousness wanders over.

"I'd really rather not." I bring Aksha into the middle of the streaming data. Segment by segment, I unspool it out. "Look, these marks are from after we left. They're from government spelunkers entering my database. But the jackhole who left this blatant mark, did you notice? Maybe he's a newbie, but tidy. If he can do this, then the only . . . "

The cat sighs.

Aksha brandishes a claw and breaks its connection to the network. I send a disconnect command, too. It's as if my stiff body is being pulled away from a warm pool. Reluctantly, I leave the network and return to harsh, cold reality. Although I feel nauseous, there are some things that are best not discussed in the network.

"Your point is that there are 'Sea Spiders' stalking us?" Aksha fidgets, grinding its claws against the hardwood floor. "Why would they do that? They have to know. We don't have anything to do with them anymore."

"I'll have to take the job to find out." I fish out the number from the chip in my head. "13330573885, Cheng Liang. Tomorrow, I'll have a chat with the university professor."

Father and Daughter

Breaking into Cheng Liang's personal computer is really easy. At 5:00 p.m., he still hasn't left work yet, but I've already worked out the man's basic situation: He has a steady job. His wife died two years ago. His daughter, Cheng Wen, is sick and recuperating at G City General Hospital. Before his daughter got sick, he barely had any interests outside of work, but after she was hospitalized, he began to search the network for everything from rumors and stories to web pages and data about "Master Hackers." They practically fill up his hard drive.

Aksha takes several pieces of data and digs into the G City General Hospital's database. We fall into our rhythm working with each other and quickly find Cheng Wen.

She is in a single-unit ICU with symptoms of schizophrenia.

She isn't manic like the other patients in the psych ward. As observed from the monitoring equipment, Cheng Wen is incredibly calm. She lies curled up on the bed. Her large, clear eyes stare at the computer at the head of the bed. According to the psych ward records, Cheng Liang installed the computer for his daughter. Without a computer, she simply stopped eating in protest.

The door opens. Cheng Liang walks in with a box lunch. A nurse stands next to him.

"Wennie?" Cheng Liang cautiously studies his daughter's response. Gently, he sets her lunch on the overbed table.

She turns her head, meeting Cheng Liang's gaze for a moment. It's not a mad glance. On the contrary, it was too calm, too still for a woman of nineteen. Her mouth opens and closes twice, as though she were saying "papa," but without any sound.

"Wennie, time to eat." Cheng Liang sits beside the bed, opens the box, careful to leave some distance between him and his daughter.

"Thank you." Courteously, she accepts the proffered lunch and takes a few elegant bites. She uses a knife and fork rather than chopsticks.

An odd feeling fills the ward. Father and daughter fall silent with each other. She's obviously his flesh and blood, but seems like a stranger, maintaining a polite distance. A fine thread of pain shone mirrorlike on their faces.

When his daughter finishes her lunch, Cheng Liang repacks the box and utensils. He stands. "I'm leaving now, Wennie."

"Oh. Goodbye," she answers.

Throughout the entire visit, she never called him her father.

I sigh, leave the hospital's monitoring system, clean up the traces of my break in, then leave the network. It's not until now that a headache pierces through my neural shield, making me dizzy and unsteady. I stagger into the kitchen, swallow a pill, and chase it down with a glass of water. Then I sit in front of my computer again.

"Don't you want to rest a bit?" Aksha asks.

"No point." I stare at the screen. "I don't need a 'full connection' for what's left. A 'machine connection' is good enough. I can guess what's going on. But what's important now is to make the university professor believe us."

“Someone who studies too much is easy to deceive.” Aksha yawns and curls into a warm ball around my leg.

About an hour later, the cell phone tracker signals: Cheng Liang has come home.

Remotely, I turn on his computer and print a line of text on his display: “Are you looking for me?”

I guess he must be scared half to death because his microphone picks up a cracking sound, as if something has been smashed to pieces.

I add: “I am a Master Hacker. You were looking for me, right? Speak. I can hear you.”

He makes a sound not unlike a strangled goose. I enable speech synthesis on his computer and start typing quickly. On his end, his speaker emits a nauseating, inhuman sound. That should be enough to make someone either hate or fear a Master Hacker.

“I know you’re looking for me,” I say. “What do you want me to do? How much are you paying? Who else knows you’re looking for a Master Hacker?”

He pants for a moment. Once he recovers: “I want . . . I want you to find someone.”

I laugh. “Find who?”

“I . . . I want you to find my daughter.” The university professor seems as helpless as a child. “I want you to find my daughter. My ‘uploaded’ daughter.”

“Your daughter hasn’t been uploaded. Right now, she is at the best hospital receiving the best possible treatment from their neurologists.” I laugh grimly.

Through his webcam, I see him back away, as if I could bite him through the network. “How . . . how did you know?”

“Because I’m a ‘Master Hacker,’” I answer.

“She isn’t my daughter!” Cheng Liang shouts. “I know she isn’t!” His hands spasm as they grip the hem of his jacket. “I know she isn’t. My daughter was uploaded. Who knows what is in her body now! I want you to find Wennie and bring her back. Money is no concern. I want her back!”

I glance over at Aksha. It yawns and nods its head.

I sigh. “Just to get this out of the way: I won’t necessarily be able find your ‘uploaded’ daughter, so I won’t ask you to pay up-front. I’ll wait until I have a lead. Naturally, I’ll be in touch. Don’t keep looking for another ‘Master Hacker.’ Otherwise, I can’t guarantee I’ll be able to pull this off. Got it?”

He nods over and over again. His cast is so desperate, it’s like he’s giving medicine to a dead horse. For a crime as serious as “uploading,” he really doesn't have any options besides looking for a "Master Hacker."

"In that case," I say slowly. "Tell me everything about what happened to your daughter."

On that side of the computer, Cheng Liang chatters endlessly with his head in his hands. On this side of the computer, I light a cigarette and listen quietly.

According to the learned university professor, his daughter was always an "obedient and well-behaved child." But, eventually, he didn't know why, she became a fan of virtual-reality games, wallowing with no way to free herself. He tried hitting her, scolding her, begging her, but none of that worked. Finally, one day, she uploaded herself, leaving her father only a brief message:

I'm exhausted.

Living up to your expectations is exhausting. Not living up to your expectations is also exhausting.

Dad, Mom, I'm sorry. Goodbye.

As a matter of fact, Cheng Wen's story and the story of everyone else who uploads themselves are all basically same. She was an only child, no siblings, and no real friends. Every day, she obediently went to school, came home afterward, ate, then slept. Home and school were the cruxes supporting a finely wrought cage. For the child inside, it seemed like the entire world.

Until one day, she became infatuated with the network.

I understand the feeling. When you go on the net, information rushes at you like a flood. It tells you that *this* is the entire world. But when you leave the net, you feel the flood waters recede. You are still in the cage. You haven't moved even a tiny step. You want that world, to enter that world, to embrace this brand new heaven and earth. You, however, discover that reality, your body, the love of your family, all weigh you down like shackles in a prison.

At a secret upload website, a sentence is written in red boldface on the home page: "When exiling humanity from paradise, God said: I will give them love." This is the best yoke. As long as they are bound by love, they will never have a way back to paradise.

This has spread among netizens. I don't know how many people try to shout from their cages. They want a new world. Actually, they are confused. A lot of people feel that the price of a new world is to lose everything in the old world. Who would make such a grave choice?

But I understand those who uploaded themselves. The reason why you abandon yourself is really simple.

Oh, yes. I understand.

For example, Cheng Wen, what she wanted was nothing more than a comparatively relaxing life. A life where there's no pressure to do well on high-stakes school entrance exams.

Another example, say there's a girl named Lin Yu. She uploaded herself because she firmly believed, in real life, she had not even one single redeeming feature. On the net, she kicked serious ass. What she did made the relatives who once thought of her as garbage respect her.

But they were both wrong. The net is not the real world. They wouldn't open their eyes in the middle of a current of electricity. They just found a piece of solid earth, clear water, and blue sky. An abyss in the net is like an ocean. It swallows everybody who throws themselves in, cleansing them.

What very few people realize: The deepest recesses of an abyss are incredibly difficult places for anyone, whether it's a program, spelunker, or Master Hacker, to reach. Huge and dismal existences hide there. It is a place where illegal data, uploaded consciousnesses, destroyed programs, and abandoned AI all mix together, lie dormant, and propagate. Some of the consciousnesses use uploaded human thoughts as a kernel. Some have only pieces of programs and evolve. They are immense, jumbled, all-embracing, and yet amount to nothing.

They call themselves "Sea Spiders."

Governments, of course, know Sea Spiders exist. They have rooted Sea Spiders out from their hiding places many times. Sea Spiders, however, are way smarter than any program, more nimble than any spelunker. They lurk like undercurrent in the net. Even the craftiest Master Hacker has a hard time detecting their existence. Because they are on the net, the likelihood of a self-reproducing consciousness is comparable to that of an infinite number of monkeys eventually typing out *Hamlet*. As a result, governments have adopted drastic measures. They've banned completely the uploading of consciousnesses, classifying it as the most serious of crimes, giving it the harshest punishment.

Of those who upload themselves, eighty percent of their consciousnesses are ripped to shreds by government web crawlers, ten percent are disintegrated into data packets, becoming rich fodder for Sea Spiders. The remaining ten percent become Sea Spiders themselves, roaming among the data, hiding from both governments and others of their own kind. They rip apart other consciousnesses to slake their thirst for data. They sniff out, even luring those who want to upload themselves, always alert to take over hollow bodies.

But only one percent of Sea Spiders luck into the bodies fools abandon to upload themselves. Those Sea Spiders return to the real world.

They are reincarnated in someone else's body.

I suppose, perhaps at the time, the woman called Cheng Wen heard a whisper in the deep recesses of the net that enticed her, called her to go. She didn't know, though, that this first step wouldn't lead to rebirth, but to eternal damnation.

Cheng Liang's hand trembles as he lights a cigarette. He tells me that one morning he opened the door to his daughter's room to see her in front of her computer, unwakeable and wearing a slight smile. He rushed her to the hospital. The doctor had to tell him: don't hold out any hope for her.

Later, as a spur-of-the-moment test, he attached her stupefied body to the network and she suddenly woke up. But the person who woke was no longer the Cheng Wen from before.

Cheng Liang enumerates exhaustively the ways she is different from before. I just let it wash over me. Because parents always have a keen intuition about their children, I believe him.

Since everyone who intends to upload hides at least one Sea Spider afterward, they hide there silently, luring and agitating. Once the uploaded consciousness leaves the mind, they race to be first to seize the already soulless body and occupy it.

As for the consciousness that leaves the body, her fate is up to one percent opportunity and ninety-nine percent luck. All she has to do is become a "Sea Spider," then follow in my footsteps to become a "Master Hacker," like I did. Easy peasy.

Cheng Liang said that he received a text: Dad, find a Master Hacker. Help me.

At the end of the text was my address. It was this text that made up his mind to admit his "daughter" to the hospital. Then he held his nose and went to the neighborhood where I'd rented an apartment.

Nowhere to Return to

By the time Professor Cheng finishes his endless narrative, it's already 4:00 a.m. My headache feels like it'll burst my head open. All sorts of random thoughts rush around and expand so that my ears buzz.

I take two pills. They help not one bit. Pissed off, I take three more. I shut down my computer. My hands pressed against my head, I sway into the kitchen and dump some tepid water onto instant noodles. I eat the half-cooked noodles, then return to my room. My bed's not made. The blanket's still unfolded. I plow in, not bothering to take off my clothes, and flop into dreamland.

It's not until 2:00 p.m. that I have the strength to crawl out of bed. I rub my face, grab some cash, then shop at the supermarket downstairs. Carrying bags and bags of snacks and cat food, I catch sight of a pay phone. A long while passes before I walk to it and dial a familiar number.

"Hello. May I ask who are you looking for?"

"Mom, it's me, Xuejiao."

Everything suddenly grows silent. Ages pass in silence. My hand trembles as I hold the handset. Not knowing where the courage is coming from, I wait and wait some more.

"Xuejiao, where are you? You changed your number again?" Mom says, finally finding the words.

"My job's been transferred to Jiaxing." I lie. I lie like this every time. Actually, I suspect she's long since figured out what I'm doing.

"Jiaxing is a good neighborhood, Xuejiao. Work hard. Look after yourself . . . " Mom's voice falls. "When . . . come on home, just to visit."

"Hm. Maybe for New Year's," I say.

Every time I promise to come home for New Year's, every time I nestle myself in my apartment, cradling Aksha. Dry-eyed, I listen to the cold New Year's bells toll. What goes through my mind is that I'm incapable of keeping my promise to my mom.

When I return, Aksha sees how listless I am and jumps onto the table. "Did you call your mom again?"

"Ugh."

Aksha licks its paws. "Aren't you just looking to make yourself depressed?"

"I am happy!" I sulk at it in return.

"If you want to cry, cry, Xuejiao." Aksha's tone implies a worldly experience undercut by the cat food stuck on its whiskers.

Shrugging, I pick up a cash-filled envelope, count out two-thirds of the money, then split that in two.

"Are you going to post the money?"

"Oh, like always. Half goes to Mom, half to Auntie Zhou." I hide the cash in a pocket.

Aksha licks my finger with its rough tongue. "Don't forget to take your medication before you go."

"I know."

After I return from the post office, Aksha and I gorge ourselves. We demolish everything I brought back from the supermarket. Then I sleep until the following morning.

On the theory that I'll need a lot of energy and physical strength to look for a "Sea Spider," I take a full dose of antirejection medication. It makes me feel like I'm sleepwalking. I shake off my blanket and change clothes. Having skipped combing my hair, washing my face, and brushing my teeth, I eat two eggs, drink a bag of milk, turn on my computer, and go online.

Cheng Liang said that his daughter lost herself in the game *Rivers and Lakes Unlimited*. Moreover, he insisted that I go into the game to look for his daughter's consciousness. Instead, I do something much simpler. I find and follow the trail of uploaded packets on the computer.

The trail breaks at the first node. That's not exactly a surprise. On the side, Aksha has already downloaded her game data and began to look for similarly skilled IDs in *Rivers and Lakes Unlimited*.

"There isn't any," it says. Scrubbed clean. They left behind fewer tracks than even the craftiest rat.

Government databases also haven't captured any records of any data packets similar to consciousnesses. "Or maybe those records been deleted," I reply.

"Where else could there be clues?" Aksha asks.

"Abysses," I answer. The deepest abysses.

It's never been easy to find any Sea Spider, let alone a specific Sea Spider. Now there are two possibilities: his daughter became a Sea Spider herself or, even worse, Sea Spiders broke her up into splintered pieces of data and integrated them into many different consciousnesses. I adjust my gear and begin to search.

Know this: "jacking in" and "uploading" feel nothing like each other. To use a particularly fitting metaphor, jacking your mind into the net is drifting along a river in a boat. Uploading your mind, however? Flinging yourself directly into the water. You have to master how to see, how to breathe, how to live in the water. Everything you know is turned completely on its head. Before you are swallowed, you have to make yourself a fish.

After I think about it a bit, I decide to start from the game. If she liked this game so much, in her ignorance, she might have clutched at this desperate straw when she first entered the world of the net.

Heading straight toward the game, I search between the node the trail broke at and the game's server node, not letting even the whisper of a clue pass me by.

Clue one: September 2nd. That's the day she uploaded. *Rivers and Lakes Unlimited* District Three Server Six, a card machine appeared, was forcibly ejected, then disconnected.

Clue two: Server Six is typically overloaded.

Clue three: A tracking program was once run from here. Objective unknown. The server was located in Wuxi. That was the city I lived in until Cheng Liang scared me into moving.

"It's here," Aksha says.

I dive in deep. The server has a series of storage areas. They are ingeniously scattered across different locations and linked together. As a whole, however, they are difficult for someone to find.

In the mind-machine interface, I open the door.

A range of golden mountains burn my eyes. Red and yellow leaves in a forest, mixed with the green of the pine. Late autumn frost smears the earth with a thin layer of white. The fields have already been harvested. Tall piles of corn lie at the edges. Golden kernels glint against the transparent, deep blue sky.

"Do you miss it? Xia Xuejiao, do you miss your home?" a thin, reluctant voice asks.

A young woman walks toward her from a low, flat-roofed house. It's Cheng Wen. With a tiny nose and round face, she is as adorable as a doll when she laughs. Her eyes, however, are black. They are as distant as the night sky and unfathomably haunted.

"Or perhaps I should call you Ji Cina?" She begins to laugh. "It's been a long time, old friend."

" . . . Jill?" I sputter and spit out the code name.

The scenery around me suddenly begins to roil. It changes into countless flows of color, like a rainbow corridor. Aksha and I are at one end. Cheng Wen is at the other.

"I've been waiting for you." She laughs and twirls. Her skirt flutters, becoming a beautiful flower. "After I 'downloaded' my consciousness into this body, that stupid girl regretted abandoning her body. Actually, she shouldn't have tracked you down. And she shouldn't have sent your address to her father. If she had just continued to hide in that server, the computer I compromised in the mental hospital would have never found her."

My heart aches.

"You stole her body. Now, you've eaten her consciousness?" I ask.

"Don't get all noble on me." Her delicate face is ice cold. "Are the things you've done any better?"

"How much of you is still Cheng Wen?"

"A lot. Almost forty percent." She gestures. "With so much data, why would I share it with anyone else? I tore her apart, ate her, and merged her data with mine. It still needs time to digest."

I look her over. There is a familiar hunger and thirst in her serene eyes. Although every Sea Spider propagates across the consciousness of those who uploaded themselves, every Sea Spider also yearns to return to reality.

"You want a body that much?" I ask softly.

"You have a body, yourself, but you stop others from getting one?" She curls her lips. "So many Sea Spiders. They're all looking for bodies to the point of abducting them. When I saw this one, I took it. What's wrong with that?"

"The day you download yourself, it's not exactly a comfortable one." I laugh bitterly.

"And yet. I want . . . I want arms that can hug. I want eyes that can cry. I want a body. I want . . . " She stays silent for a long time. "I want to go home."

When one Sea Spider swallows another Sea Spider, their personalities merge. In that moment, I can't tell them apart. The one who wants to go home, is it the one who has been flowing in the abyss for a long time, who long ago abandoned a corporeal existence? Or is it the girl who foolishly rushed into the net with no way to return?

"It's not so easy," I say. "Even if you've stuffed the immense 'Sea Spider' consciousness into a brain, you'll have to take black-market drugs to prevent consciousness rejection for the rest of your life. Also, how are you going to leave the mental hospital?"

"That's none of your business," she says.

"Suit yourself," I answer. "I have one final question I want to ask."

"Go ahead." Jill—Cheng Wen shrugs. "Quickly. The nurses are making their rounds."

"You said you want to go home. But to whose home? Jill Lenk's home in America, in Kansas? Or Cheng Wen's home in Shanghai?"

She's silent, dumbfounded for a long time. She raises her head then, disappointed, gazes at me with her black, serene eyes.

"I . . . I don't know."

Satisfied, I laugh. Step-by-step, I leave this abyss. When it's time for me to break the connection, Jill—Cheng Wen's sigh flutters in the distance.

"Ji Cina, which home can you return to?"

A sharp pain pierces my chest. The javelin I hurt her with turned around and penetrated into my own feelings. Fragments of the city of fluttering, thin light rain in the midst of mansions and skyscrapers and the peaceful village within the range of snow-crested mountains twist together. They remain choked in my throat.

"Mama . . . " I mutter to myself.

I have no idea who I'm calling for. Lin Yu's mother or mine.

Mother

I was in college when I uploaded myself. A first-class fool at the time, I followed a man I had a crush on into the net. Only then did I realize I was no more than a tasty morsel of flesh. I have no idea what the man's sorry fate was. In the rush of data, I couldn't find any fragment of him or any tracks leading to him.

I ran in the abyss, dodging government programs. At the same time, I was hiding from or killing my kind, swallowing their data to replenish myself. "Ji Cina" was a name I adopted out of convenience. It means nothing to me. Just three syllables you squeeze out with your tongue pressed against your teeth, terse and fierce.

Sea Spiders almost always break off contact completely with their new bodies' friends and relatives. However, I've heard of those who could return to their former life. I don't know where the person who took my body went. Her trail ends in Australia. I've been very careful, never entering that relatively unfamiliar section of the net.

In the local net, for the longest time, Jill and I tangled with each other. We fought, trying to swallow each other. Ultimately, though, we set our boundaries, defining our spheres of influence. No one was more fierce and ruthless than I was. Crazed, I plundered all the data for a chance to return to the real world. In the fight among Sea Spiders for bodies, though, opportunities were fleeting.

Until the day I met Aksha.

Aksha was actually small and weak. Compared to our group of "Sea Spiders," it lacked mobility and flexibility. However, it wasn't encumbered by so much excess data. "Sea Spiders" generally retain data about the body, ready, just in case, for that day when they returned to the real world. Since it's an AI, Aksha doesn't have any of that. It being in an abyss is like a stranded fish returned to the water. As if it were a rat aside our big elephant feet.

It told me that it wanted a body. It, however, wasn't compatible with human bodies.

"I think I have a solution," I said. "Let's make a deal."

When a new consciousness emerged confused among us, with Aksha's help, I detoured around the chaotic fight. I penetrated directly into the empty brain.

The rejection response was more violent than I'd imagined. For a week after getting the body, I lay in a hospital bed, mournfully wailing through my mental and physical trial. It wasn't until Aksha brought me a fragment of consciousness it snatched from the net that my condition improved.

Two days after I left the hospital, I found an excuse to leave the family of the woman called Lin Yu. From the black market, I stole a huge supply of antirejection drugs, an upload-download unit, as well as a yellow cat whose intelligence was augmented by a microchip.

Since then, I've brought Aksha along. We began our roving days.

In these last few years, in my pocket is invariably hidden a letter. It was written by a mother to her daughter who was already never going to return.

My dearest Yu:

It's been so long since I've heard any news of you.

Mom knows you're doing your best out there, building your career. But since you can't come home for New Year's, you're never home at all.

I miss you. Your father also speaks of you.

You're an adult now. You should find a man to marry.

This year, why don't you come back to Pudong for a short visit. Don't make us worry. You don't need to send us so much money. Your father's and my pensions are enough.

Mom, Zhou Yun

2075/1/26

I raise my head. In the mirror is a healthy woman, wrinkled pajamas wrapped around her, unkempt hair, bluish-black eyes. A small mole dots the corner of my mouth.

Every time I look at myself in the mirror I feel strange. It's as if Lin Yu's family in Shanghai, Lin Yu's mother, her taciturn father, not to mention the Shanghainese that I understand not one word of, they constantly warn me: I'm actually a thief who stole someone else's body.

The day I left Lin Yu's family, her mother opened an umbrella and saw me off to the end of the lane. She already realized by then that someone else's soul occupied Lin Yu's body, but she still smiled. She still tried to convince the incomplete likeness of her daughter to stay.

She sent this letter four years ago to my first address. I moved immediately after. Drifting about, I've never had any news of her. I never write my address on any money order I post. Frequently, though, I see the silhouette of her going from house to house knocking on doors, and I have no choice but to sneak out the back door in a rush.

The Lin Yu who uploaded herself, the fragment I received of her is actually not very large. In my bones, I am still the "Sea Spider" Xin Xuejiao. My mother is still the woman waiting in a small town in the Northeast Forest District. As for Lin Yu, I received her body, but not a way to love her family.

Return Home, Return Home

New Year's Eve, I carry Aksha with me to the train station. There's a missing person notice stuck to the station entrance. It rustles in the breeze.

Missing Person Notice:
Cheng Wen, female, 19 years old.
Wearing a cream-colored sweater, white overcoat, black jeans. Long hair. Wears glasses.
Disappeared on 2079/1/6.
I hope a good-hearted person will provide a clue.
I hope my daughter will return home.
Father Cheng Liang weeping 2079/1/10.

Speechless, I study the grainy picture printed on the notice. Cheng Wen's smile gives one a feeling of distance. Yet another Sea Spider who didn't realize until after returning to this world that there is nowhere to leave for, but also nowhere to return to.

I laugh bitterly. Holding Aksha, I board the train back to my hometown in the Northeast.

The hometown I left six years ago looks just like it used to. Tiny towns seem to freeze in time. Only the people who live in them slowly grow old. Clinging to a thread of hope, I plucked up my courage to return here.

Auntie Zhou and Cheng Liang, they could realize someone else's consciousness lived in the body of their child. On the other hand, can my mother pierce through the Yin Yu exterior and see what I used to look like? Even if she hugs me, will she still call me Xuejiao?

I put on my overcoat and pick up Aksha. The warmth of its body gives me a bit of courage.

"Just give it a go," it says.

"Hm."

I leave the hotel. The harsh northeast wind carves my face. On the road, at the edge of town, my mother is waiting for her daughter to return for New Year's.

I muster my courage and walk toward my mom. It's been so many years since I've seen her. She is old now. Her thick down jacket seems empty wrapped around her gaunt body. She is curled up against the cold wind, a pair of cloudy eyes stubbornly facing front, waiting for me to return home.

I'm back, Mom.

I walk over. And I keep walking. Her gaze slides past my body. My steps grazed her. What she sees is an unfamiliar woman carrying a cat. Who I brush past is my mother.

The wind and snow flutter, turning heaven and earth pure white. My mother and I are two tiny black dots on the white ground. The more I walk, the farther away I go. The more I walk, the farther away I go.

I don't know how many bodies carry other peoples' souls. I don't know how many mothers wait in vain for their children to come home.

You have eyes that can shed tears, but not necessarily eyes that can cry.

You have arms that can hug, but not necessarily arms that can hug the people you love.

Originally published in Chinese in *Science Fiction World,* May 2006.

Translated and published in partnership with Storycom.

ABOUT THE AUTHOR

Chi Hui was born in northeast China. She has been an editor and writer for *Science Fiction World,* China's premiere genre magazine. She has garnered numerous nominations and honors, including a 2016 Chinese Nebula Silver Award for her novel *Artificial Humanity 2075: Recombined Consciousness.*

Forward Momentum and a Parallel Toss

ANAMARIA CURTIS

On the marching band field, everything echoes of Alex. Lacey's students spread across the sideline and cue their robots, and Lacey sees herself as a teenager in a giant sweatshirt, Alex next to her, looks at the bots and remembers Alex's head on hers when she curled up around him in the last row of the bus, talking through choreography. But those are the wrong kinds of memories to have of Alex, so Lacey swallows down nostalgia and focuses on the field, looking for tiny errors to focus on at the next practice. They're going to win regionals today, but state will be harder.

The robots roll onto the field, music swelling from speakers, each robot an individual instrument, and she looks for Edsel and Amber, each on one end of the line of students, wearing their blue cocaptain armbands, holding the manual override controls. To the left of Amber is Bruin, in his yellow and green JM sweatshirt and baseball cap, shoulders straight, and Lacey sees Alex there too, the unfortunate heart of the problem she was never able to solve.

She sits in the stands, unusual for a coach, but everyone has their whims, and watches her students absolutely steamroll over the competition. Their bass drums have real arms and drums instead of speakers, and twelve of their robots can do a parallel toss, their long, oddly-jointed arms making precise work of the back-to-front transition and the proud whirl of color overhead. The other teams have no chance.

They'll have to stay for the exhibition performance now, which Lacey resents despite herself, but the exhibition is all the kids—she doesn't even know what its final form looks like—so she sneaks off to get some ice cream while they're preparing for it.

As she goes to pay, a man in a long-sleeved JM shirt puts his sundae next to hers and says he's paying, and Lacey turns to argue, but then she sees it's Alex.

"What the hell are you doing here?" she asks, when they're safely in a deserted high school hallway, invisible to the teams scurrying around to pack up and prepare for the awards and exhibition. Her ice cream is melting into its biodegradable bowl.

"I volunteered to be a JM recruiter for regionals," he says. "Hoped to catch you and thought the ice cream stand was my surest bet." His grin unfurls like an open secret, and for a second Lacey doesn't begrudge him being right.

But mostly seeing him just makes her sad. "What do you want, Alex?"

And just like that the grin is gone. "I wanted to warn you to settle down a little," he says, sticking his thumb through a belt loop, looking anywhere but at her. "JM sales in Madrid"—he winks—"comma Illinois, have been going down since you came back and started coaching the band, and now some people are trying to get out of their contracts early. I don't want to have to do any digging into the reason why, but you understand I have my suspicions." He says "Madrid" like a local, the A pronounced long and flat as in apple.

"JM's a big company. I don't think a few counties buying less equipment is going to wreck your profit margins."

Alex chews on his lip, and Lacey reads it all on his face. JM's weaker than it looks. All the sales matter to them right now.

"Competition?" She offers after a moment. "Trouble in corporate paradise?"

Alex scowls and avoids the question. "Everyone in Madrid is growing vegetables, Lacey. And you and I both know people aren't planting acres of carrots and beets by hand."

She shrugs. "They could be. I don't know much about planting." A lie. She's learned a lot the last few years. "Honestly, Alex, 'the band' is literally just twenty-some teenagers looking to practice coding and make robots do funny stuff with their metal limbs. We're no threat."

"All I'm saying is, it would look a lot better if some of the kids from the band were a little more interested in JM contracts. It's good money. And it would help if the sales numbers in the area went up."

"And if they don't?"

There are bags under Alex's eyes and lines on his forehead. He exudes weariness. When he speaks, it's with a sadness that makes Lacey think of a seed, buried deep in dark blocks of soil, of fingers beyond its control pressing it into place.

"Then JM's going to investigate, and they're going to find something, and they're going to prosecute the hell out of it." He sighs. "They've given you a folder, a number. You're a project now. We used to be friends, Lace. I don't want to see you in jail."

She maneuvers around the "used to" in her head, the weighty factuality of it, the pang it gives her. A little corner of her mind compares it to the sound of her nickname from his mouth.

Alex hands her a business card. "Call me if you have any questions."

"It was good of you to let me know," she says.

Lacey thinks through it on the bus home. Behind her, two dozen of her high school students are huddled up against each other, talking and laughing and sleeping on each other's shoulders. These are the coziest memories of her own time in robotics marching band a decade ago, sharing a seat with Alex, watching old Drum Corps videos they'd saved on their tablets, trying to come up with new ideas, or just giggling at ridiculous old jokes, gleeful and easily amused with exhaustion.

Lacey's always known this was going to happen. She didn't think she'd hear it from Alex himself, but she knew. JM has tech, and JM has plenty of connections with the cops, in Illinois and all over, and JM has a small army of lawyers. That's why her notes and drawings are all in neatly organized paper notebooks, her files with scanned copies encrypted and secured under a fake name online, why she insists people call her if they have questions about their robots instead of emailing. But that could only get her so far.

She could slow things down for a while. Or she could leave. It's what she's always planned on doing, eventually. Edsel and Amber (and Schuyler and probably Rose and maybe Mason) know enough to help keep people's machines in order, and they're smart and eager and they get why it's important. At least, she thinks they do. They're good kids, but that's a lot to put on them. Too much.

If she leaves, Madrid will slip in JM's priorities. Maybe that's safer for everyone.

But. JM's weak at the moment. She can dig into it later—could be some expansion to the west coast has them overextended, or some investments abroad—but she should be using it. She needs to speed up, not slow down.

And that was always the fundamental difference between Alex and her, wasn't it. It was a stupid risk to steal the backup robots and reprogram and reoutfit them to do her chores on the farm in high school, and it was an even bigger one to go to college. For Alex, going to work for JM was safe, and since his parents were still tens of thousands of dollars in debt on their combine, the employee assistance was just a bonus.

Lacey left but swore she'd come back, for Madrid, for Alex, for every problem she didn't know how to solve yet. She made friends in college, the kind she could come back to, the kind who traded ideas with her late at night and didn't back down from them in the morning, but she was always going to leave them.

It's dark outside, but the bus sways on, and Lacey can tell they're nearing Madrid because the fields aren't tagged with illuminated IP labels anymore, and solar houses with herbs and vegetables loom like strange translucent creatures on the edge of her vision. It's strange, she thinks, that the more she does, the closer she gets, the less Madrid looks like the town she grew up in, the town she missed so much.

When Lacey returned to Madrid three years after college, she came with enough equipment from her dead start-up to fill two barns. By then, Alex was long gone, on the other side of a divide Lacey didn't know how to start crossing.

But Lacey wants him back, and she wants what's best for her town, and she knows that now's the time. She has to make her play.

Lacey's team has three weeks until state. Thousands of people will come to watch the winning teams perform, to mill around the JM campus and stadium, to buy from food trucks and watch seed shows. For high schoolers, there's the job fair. JM will continue their streak, snapping up the most promising candidates for their four-year training rotations and overpaid engineering jobs that leave workers trapped up in NDAs and noncompetes and too much information to be useful somehow, overselling DRM-locked equipment that only works on their seeds. Not that Lacey's biased.

She is working hard, as are her students. From 7:30 a.m. to 6:00 p.m., the band's machines are all theirs, and Lacey takes advantage of this by adding early morning practices to after-school time. Her students show up yawning, with coffee and tea in thermoses that they pretend to feed to their machines. Marching robots are roughly composed of a box on wheels, speakers, and some combination of brightly painted limbs, but most students draw marker faces with angry eyebrows or goofy smiles on the upper box. Schuyler and Mason work on balance and flexibility on the wheels and, after hours of hard work, achieve the first robot wheelie south of I-80. With this kind of talent and dedication, Lacey thinks they can't lose.

Each kid has three robots under their control, sometimes four or five for the upperclassmen. With their machines, it's not so much a matter of precision—that's the norm—but of cohesion and flair. They got third at state last year, but Lacey is counting on winning this year. Her robots' fake wrists can turn and loop; their fingers can grab with varying degrees of pressure, and this makes them the best color guard at state—in any division.

Those fake wrists and dexterous fingers make them useful for moving soil blocks, too, for prodding seeds into little wells and packing soil down on top. They keep track of watering schedules as well as musical scores—better, really—and the tilling attachments that fit on the trumpet section come in handy in late spring. And that's why, when her students go home after practice every day, most of them take a machine with them, rolling alongside their bikes or pressed, compact, in the back of their cars. After they leave, Lacey puts the rest in her pickup and takes them to a few drop-off spots: the corner between Lillian Wang's greenhouses and Salem Lester's sweet corn patch, surrounded by solar fence because of the damned raccoons, the park in the town center, the gravel lot between Tracy King's cow field and Kevin Chanhira's apricot and apple orchard.

Between 6:00 p.m. and 7:30 a.m., people can do whatever they want with the marching machines, as long as they've talked to Lacey first and have them charged by the end. She teaches a Saturday afternoon class on weekends they're not practicing, going over the basics of what machines are and aren't capable of, how they're fixed, what instructions they need,ay and how they use the information.

The other teams at state won't have been sharing machines with anyone, let alone farms, but Lacey thinks it's an advantage. Over the past four years she's been coaching the band, she's found that what's good for the plants is usually good for the band too.

Lacey's building more machines, still, with her own money and the parts from the barns. She has diagrams for dozens more. She was planning on starting to sell them at cost this summer, instructions and diagrams included. Now she'll have to get it all set up within weeks.

She doesn't know how much of a difference it'll make. Even though the JM office in Madrid has downsized, the ones a couple counties over are doing just fine. Everyone there is still growing corn and soybeans like their parents, locked in debt cycles they ignore with Midwestern stoicism.

Lacey has a JM tractor of her own in the machine shed behind the barn. It's an old model, inherited, but it can already do a lot more than plant patented corn and soybeans.

• • •

Lacey comes into morning practice a little later than usual one morning, swearing at herself for leaving her tea on the kitchen counter. That's why it takes her a minute to see the row of teenagers crossing their arms at her.

"What's happening?" she asks, immediately running through a list of emergency scenarios in her head. "What's wrong?"

"You're working too hard on this project for state," Schuyler says, handing Lacey a cup of coffee. "We're going to help."

Lacey takes a sip and grimaces at the taste. "That's very kind," she says, "but I don't know what you're talking about."

The five of them present her with their evidence. Notes she left on her desk with formation diagrams, late nights, some code she fed to a marcher and forgot to replace with the standard. Nothing strong enough to get her in trouble, but enough dots for smart kids to connect.

"If you know what this is about," she says, "you know this could be dangerous. You'll lose any chance of a job with JM. They may be able to blacklist you." She swallows. "Full disclosure, they might try to have me arrested. They might succeed."

"We'll be okay," Edsel says, poised as always. "We'll mostly focus on the exhibition. Stick to the legal stuff where we can."

Lacey fidgets. "My plan isn't perfect. It's barely even formed. Is that really worth risking your futures over?"

Amber gestures at the workroom, and she seems to encompass everything—the wind kites on the roof, the graying walls, the smallness of it all. "What futures, really? Most of us are going to stay here after we graduate and farm or raise animals. The robots are our best bet. If we don't do something, if we just keep moving along until someone stops us, we'll be back in JM's showrooms, signing away what we don't even have."

"And," Edsel adds. "I read an article about JM being in trouble with a lender because of some faulty investments they made in West Africa. Now's the best chance we've got."

"It's not fair that any of this should be on you," she says.

Amber shrugs. "Life's not fair. JM's business model isn't fair. We should still try."

It seems too easy to say it like that, but maybe she's right. Lacey could use the help, and they're offering. They've been paying more attention than she realized. It's their town too. "Okay," Lacey says. "You want to use the exhibition if we win?"

They all nod.

"Do you have a plan for it?"

Schuyler grins. "My understanding is that we have to make the biggest, most attention-grabbing scene we can and then throw information at them until they can't ignore it." He throws an arm around Mason. "Lemme tell you, Ms. Clemmens, Mason and I are great at making a scene."

Mason nods. "Our genuine specialty."

That's at least worth a smile. "They could find a way to wave it away," she offers, a last feeble attempt.

"Not if we make it big enough!"

"But—"

"No buts," Rose says. She's always been quiet, but she looks Lacey in the eye. "We want to help." She shrugs, knowing her point is won. "And your odds are better if we do."

"This is the most irresponsible thing I have ever done," Lacey says, and then she starts explaining how they're going to do it.

Lacey is too impulsive for her own good and too stubborn by far. Everyone's always said it. This must be why she calls Alex the Saturday morning a week before state. They're halfway through a mark-by-mark run-through, and the kids have gone inside to get water and battery packs and more jar lids, and she's working on an actuator that's been rolling its triple twist too quickly.

Lacey pauses to check the instructions, in a picture on her phone, and the picture of Alex's business card is right next to it, his number auto-scanned into her contacts. She presses the linked number and hits "call" before she can lose her nerve.

"Hi, Lacey," Alex's voice sounds almost warm on the phone.

She closes her eyes. "You shouldn't know what my phone number is."

"Ah, well. What can I help you with?"

Lacey swallows. His calls—and hers, if she's being honest—are probably being recorded. "It was kind of you to talk to me when we ran into each other a few weeks ago. I wanted to return the favor."

"What?"

"Alex," Lacey says his name like an anchor, lets it sink into the silence. "Is this what you really want? To work for JM forever? Because, listen. I'm going to . . . keep going with this. With what we discussed." She pauses, considering. "I want you to help me. Help me with it, help me get away with it, whatever."

She hears his hissed intake of breath.

"You shouldn't have told me that."

"I trust you," she says. "I think you're better than this." It's mostly true.

"I'll see you on Saturday, Lace."

• • •

Lacey and her five students work beyond the extra hours the whole team is already putting in. She orders them pizza three nights in a row, and then, beset by guilt, brings in salads and containers of radishes, turnips, and carrots from her greenhouse, most of which are politely ignored.

Edsel and Amber are in charge of the extra robots, the ones that don't have to meet the competition specifications because they aren't for the competition. Once they finish the choreography, Schuyler and Mason work on the website, researching the environmental effects of monocultures and herbicide-resistant genetics and arguing over how they're going to format their citations. Lacey stops what she's doing sometimes to give them a monologue about the ethics of IP law, which they nod at and ignore because they already wrote that whole page and she's not telling them anything they don't already know.

Lacey grins to herself sometimes on these late nights, thinking about how much these kids care, watching them do the work. The glow of computer screens and flat overhead lighting lights up their space in the shop, and Lacey's water heater is bubbling in the background, the smell of tea and coffee mixing with motor oil. They don't talk much, hunched over their computers or their robots, but they're connected all the same.

Rose works on the pamphlet, the scan codes for the website, the graphics. She goes outside one evening and throws paper around in the wind, different shapes and sizes, different weights. Somehow this turns into a spreadsheet she and Cass are working on, weighing the benefits and drawbacks of their paper options, and then Cass is there too on the nights when she doesn't have to take care of the animals, shrugging herself around Rose like a favorite cardigan.

They leave the diagrams for Lacey to fret over. She brings parts into the shop to take pictures of on the grimy concrete floor and considers sketching them out instead. She stares at the JM logo, carefully stamped on each individual part, and thinks about how illegal it all is.

And that's the other side of the work they're doing, the fear. When she's getting in the middle of Schuyler and Mason's argument about citation styles or timing the seconds it takes two pieces of confetti to fall from equal heights for Rose, it hits her hard, like hands around her rib cage, around her throat. These kids are *kids*. She's doing the diagrams, she's directing them, she's careful that they not put anything in writing or online. They probably won't go to jail, but the black mark they're putting on their futures will be all too real, and she won't be able to protect them, won't even be around.

But then again, most of them are seniors. Next year, a couple of them might head to college, but most of them are going to be in Madrid, same as ever. Lacey remembers being in high school—in this high school, in this town—all too well. She thinks she's stuck in parallels sometimes, the past, present, and hoped-for future a constant relay in her head. But she needs to put behind the fond ghosts of the past and work in the moment for the future as she envisions it—a community growing a range of crops, working on the technology together, free of the looming shadow of corporate debt.

That's what Lacey wants for her students. Even better, they want more for themselves. They'll protect each other, she knows.

They leave for state at 5:00 a.m., Lacey ushering yawning students into the bus, checking that they have all their tools. They settle into seats quietly, pulling sweatshirts and blankets over themselves. Lacey is wide awake, nearly vibrating with anxiety. She checks the code on her laptop, checks her bag for oil and spare parts. She talks to the bus driver, a formality given the self-driving mechanism, and straightens the cuffs on her sweater. This kind of nervous energy usually dissipates once she's done what she needs to; today it lingers. Back at her house, her car is packed. Once they're back in Madrid she's heading east, the fastest way out of JM's stronghold. She'll stay with college friends, pick up the language of start-ups and cities again, keep moving.

So Lacey looks out the window and watches for the first signs of daylight washing over the sky in creeping pastels, watches the sun rise and spread long shadows over the fields. The farther they go, the more corn and soybeans she sees, identifiable by the IP labels on the fences. She starts counting telephone poles.

The nervous energy follows her all day. She takes it to setup and check in, where they take a classroom for their machines and warm them up, but by the time it's time for them to actually perform, it's been replaced by a kind of exhausted calm. She watches her students walk up to the judges and bow, a relatively steady line of jeans and dark blue T-shirts, and clear the field. The drum major robot starts, a particular point of pride, and creates its own stand. It bows to the judges and salutes while the rest of the robots take their positions, the color guard rolling different flags to the front beforehand. The drum major's first finger extends into a long baton, and it starts the performance.

Lacey isn't entirely present in her body for the performance, just conscious of the press of her fingers on her palms and the pulse of the beat in her mind. Everything happens when it should, the flags slicing across the air like morning sunbeams, the music swelling at the end, the marchers' feet lined up. She surges up with the rest of the crowd when it ends, clapping and whistling before she's aware that she's adding to the din.

When they announce the scores an hour later, she's not surprised that they've won—in their tiny division—but she still cries a little. She gives the kids a few hours of freedom while she and her core students wander back to their classroom and start to set up for the exhibition.

Alex strolls by an hour in, his green and yellow shirt practically glowing. He congratulates the kids and mentions that if they haven't checked out the career opportunities in the JM showroom, he's sure they'll still be open after the exhibition, for the winners. He mentions he met one of their teammates, a nice young man named Bruin, but hasn't seen anyone else from Madrid.

"Thanks, sir," Amber says, her brown eyes boring into him like the lasers Lacey has always dreamed of installing on her bots, "but we're not interested."

Lacey tenses. Alex pauses, resting his weight on one foot, threading his thumbs into the pockets of his jeans, and takes in what he's seeing. Lacey and six of her students looking frazzled and working hard on robot arms, angling their screens away from him, hours before the exhibition.

"Alright," he says. "Good luck to you. Looks like we're going to have our biggest crowd yet."

It's that pose. The lean, the polite conversational deflection. Lacey looks at him, and for a moment she's fifteen, and she finally has a friend, and he's funny and doesn't break Kit Kats before eating them. And she's eighteen, and he's moving to Peoria to start his job, and she hugged him before, but now his parents are there, so he extends a hand and tells her to take care of herself. And she's twenty at a New Year's Eve party, finally home for a break, and so excited to see Alex that she tells him everything at once—what JM's doing, the stuff she's learning about, all the ways she wants to try to fix it—and he smiles at her, too polite, and says something about the weather.

Lacey's not going to lose the battle and the war. She wants her friend back.

Alex texts her a few minutes later, *Don't do this.*

You could come with me.

The exhibition show starts at eight, and as the winners of the smallest division, they go first. Lacey watches the stadium fill, sections full of people in green and yellow baseball caps, sections of farmers taking an evening off to come see the future of agricultural technology and talent.

At 8:07, the stadium lights dim, and field lights flood the pitch. Lacey watches as Schuyler and Rose move from teammate to teammate slowly, unobtrusively, somehow missing Bruin. They're explaining the new plan for the exhibition.

The drum major enters, sets its stand, bows, and salutes. The color guard flags are red, but some of the other machines have flags too, in yellow and green. As the drum major starts the piece, the marchers with yellow and green flags move smoothly into position, forming the letters J and M. The crowd cheers.

The color guard, red flags waving, move into a tight circle around the JM, then in a diagonal line across it. They begin to slowly rotate around the circle, each marcher raising its red flag to connect in the diagonal as it reaches the crucial point. The music swells; the crowd goes silent. Everyone is leaning in, looking at the field, taking pictures, mouths gaping.

Lacey releases a small marcher next to her in the stands and watches it roll through the crowds and hop up the stairs on plastic feet. From where they're sitting below, Edsel and Amber and Schuyler will be doing the same. She knows where they're headed, to four different corners of the stadium, and she waits for a moment, enough to take one long breath. When the music swells again—there—she anticipates before she sees the confetti in the air.

The audience doesn't know whether to clap, but people do grab at the pieces of paper, waterproof, eighty pounds, and square because that's what Rose decided. Lacey watches as people frown at the words and the scan code, as they pull out their phones. Some of them take pictures of the diagrams on the back, instructions for a basic field model to be constructed out of parts removable from a locked JM machine.

Lacey's about to be in a lot of trouble.

But in this moment, she has anonymity. She's just another person in the stands watching the remains of a monumental mistake. She watches Amber hug Mason as Edsel pumps his fists. They're giddy with it, what feels like victory. Fear trickles down her throat into her chest. She thinks they're safe, but she can't be sure.

There's an audible hum rising through the crowd now that the music has stopped—of excitement and interest, she hopes. She hopes and hopes that the people in the stands want to look at fields and see opportunity and bright colors in a variety of crops. In the box across the stadium, JM executives are jumping to their feet. One of them is scratching his head. Most of the others are pulling out their phones, gesturing angrily at each other. In this, and in the hum of interest, Lacey snatches at victory.

Lacey's notebooks have been disseminated. Edsel and Amber know almost everything anyway, and they know how to get in contact with her if necessary. JM can't destroy everything. A smile pulls at the side of her face, and she lets it unroll into a grin.

To her right, Alex is walking toward her, gently moving people out of his way. He could be coming to let her slip out of his fingers or to run away with her. He could be coming to detain her. She thinks she can hear his footsteps alone amid the din. Perhaps it's just her heartbeat.

She doesn't quite want to look at his face. She finds she can't bear it, at the end, to know whose side he's on.

ABOUT THE AUTHOR

AnaMaria Curtis is from the part of Illinois that is very much not Chicago. She's the winner of the 2019 Dell Magazines Award and enjoys starting fights about 19th century British literature and getting distracted by dogs. You can find her on Twitter at @AnaMCurtis.

Songs of Activation

ANDY DUDAK

1

Pinander has been reciting "Song of Manifold Suns"all morning, in overgrown, forgotten garden nooks or neglected library aisles, far from the mutterings of other desperate students. Ancient knowledge comes to life within him. By lunch, he understands complex marvels:

The finer ethical justifications of the empire, as worked out by the ancients.

The properties of quantized space-time, which make it the ultimate data storage medium, and allow it to be manipulated, colonized, and settled.

In moments like these, the looming exam holds no fear for him.

The Grand Arcade is full of other black-robed students by the time he arrives. The usual hubbub is subdued with the exam so close. Students quietly read or recite, fueling their brains with broth.

Pinander's mind expands with activated Lore. He sits with Jain and Philo.

"Alright?"

A penitent Jain hunches over her steaming bowl.

Philo studies a scroll. "I'm not going to make it," he says.

"Where are you?" Pinander says.

"The Temple Odes."

Pinander explains the Temple Odes were songs. "Some verse lends itself to silent reading, but not the Odes. You should be reciting or singing."

Jain giggles in her soup steam.

Pinander reckons Philo is doomed. Intelligence goes a long way in the imperial service exam, but shyness can hobble you. There are soundproofed study rooms for students like Philo, but to pass the exams you must study constantly: at meals, in showers, in the loo, to and from study groups, as you drift off to sleep. There's a lot of verse like the Odes. If you don't recite or sing, Lore will go un-activated, remaining useless noise in your skull.

The years in upload aestivation will be for nothing.

"We're dropping fast now," Jain says. Her face is nearly in the porridge, her shoulders heaving with silent laughter.

2

Pinander hurries along the colonnade, whispering "Quantum Pioneers" as he goes. Each verse internalized means more activated Lore. The brutalist cliff face of the aestivation facility—dubbed "The Crypt" by students—looms over campus. Pinander recalls emerging from a seven-year dream-time in that place, the profound sense of loss. He was still ignorant when the nurses wheeled him into daylight. There was a peculiar weight on his thoughts, strange expectations and voids. He couldn't access the years of data in his skull.

3

They hear Philo has killed himself. He's one of four across campus that night.

"We're dropping fast now," Jain reiterates, high on study enhancement, rolling in the glowing fungi of the faculty garden.

"Let's go!" Pinander hisses.

She told him where she was going. He tried to talk her out of it. "Come with me or don't," she said, and of course he followed her, as always.

"We learn the classics," she says, "poetry, philosophy, for what?"

He can't get her out of here by force. He'll have to argue well: "Our educations."

"You mean activated Lore. Uploads activated by Odes, and Epics and Songs."

"Lore given context."

"It's a scam." She props herself on an elbow, glowing, staring up at him. "It's a scam, Pin, and I can't take it anymore."

"Please. You'll be the last of us to wash out."

"Philo was the best of us, and he's gone."

"He's gone because he was a selfish git!"

They were the Mercenary Three. They swore oaths to each other, and now the covenant is broken. Jain is right. Philo was the best of them. Pinander kneels and plucks a luminous fruiting body from the garden. It disintegrates between his fingers, spore illuminating the faculty square.

Professors open windows and shriek obscenities.

"Fuck the lot of you!" Jain screams. "You're all complicit! And you know what I'm talking about!" She turns to Pinander. The bio-gloaming renders her demonic. "I think they'll take me away now. There's something you should know."

"I love you too!"

"No . . . what? Listen. There's a poet they don't want us to know about. A different context for the Lore."

There has only ever been one context. Pinander struggles to digest this. "How's that possible?"

"She was on the council that coded the Lore. They eventually deemed her a counterrevolutionary. They executed her, but not before she could . . . "

The campus police are inside the compound, blaring commands amid rolling submission gas.

"There's a scroll floating around campus," Jain says. "A selection of her verse. I think that's what got to Philo in the end. Her poetry."

"You both knew about this?" Pinander says, hurt.

"We didn't want to distract you. We thought you had the best chance of passing. One of the Three had to. But we were wrong. You might be the only one of us who can handle it."

"Handle what?"

"The dichotomy, the dual mind . . . having both contexts in your skull at once. Maybe it was meant to be you all along. Fuck graduating, anyway. No one should graduate from this place."

The police close in, dispelling the garden-glow with floodlight. Pinander drops to his knees. Jain stares into the nearest police torch, her pupils shrinking to pinpoints. "I don't regret it. The physics kept me going. The grand mystery of it all. She puts it in a new light."

"The physics too? Not just the philosophy?"

"Yes, her name is Sinecure."

He's heard the name on the lips of classmates. He assumed it was a new pop idol, one of many things he doesn't have time for that his rich classmates do.

"There's just one copy of the scroll?"

"As far as I know. Philo gave it to me. I read it and passed it along to Ivier."

"And Ivier offed himself . . . two days ago?"

"You could try his girlfriend Raff."

"Since when were they together?" Gossip, another strange pastime of moneyed students.

"Submit!" an officer shouts.

4

In interface audit you see what you really are. You hide nothing from them or yourself. Pinander has always found it cathartic, unfashionable as that is.

"You're a fascist," Jain once said, "or at least a fucking sheep."

"I'm a pragmatist."

"You have no moral compass," Philo observed.

They were on the Grand Arcade, the Mercenary Three together again. But this is the past, dredged up by audit.

"I'm just trying to get ahead," Pinander replied, as he often did. "I can't afford your ideals." That always shut them up.

5

He stumbles across the quad in post-audit daze, wondering if Jain made it all up. She said all kinds of things recently. He assumed it was standard pre-exam washout, but maybe it was her new context for the empire and physics. It's hard for him imagine such perspectives, on physics of course, but more so on the empire, on its revolution and great Emanation.

"Space-time," she said in amazement, "is quantized. There are particles of space-time. Our empire has that much right."

Pinander wonders why they let him go. He must have been audit-confirmed as nonthreatening. He's relieved to be walking free, but also a tad insulted. He loves Jain. Aren't they worried he'll raise trouble over her arrest? Is he really such a benign creature? They say audits can't lie.

"You're looking out of sorts, Pin."

Professor Wigh looms before him in her scandalously tattered robe. Her eyes are severe behind a screen of unkempt gray hair. "Don't tell me you're washing out."

"I'm on a constitutional."

"Then march back to the gardens and sing Odes. They're important to foundational physics as well as political theory. You're hardly a model pupil."

"I do what I can, under financial pressure most students here couldn't imagine."

"Precisely why I think you can beat them, in the end. Stop loitering and get to it."

Pinander looks up at stacked worlds of orange-glowing cloud. Wigh follows his gaze and asks, "What do you see?"

"A poisonous atmosphere . . . an invisible shield keeping it bay."

"Epic thirty-seven, verse fourteen, would activate Lore on that. And you'll need more for an exam essay. That invisible shield, for instance, is a spin foam hack. How about the Darkling Sea?"

She means the body of methane surrounding the university's island. Pinander looks down at the lichenous tundra turf of the quad, then toward The Crypt and Arcade and dormitories, his little universe. "If you're so concerned about my academic performance, how about a tip?"

"I think I just gave you one."

"I mean insider stuff. Aren't you on the exam committee?"

"I've never had a student ask me to help them cheat before." Wigh chuckles. "I'm sorry, Pin. I haven't been surprised by anything in quite a while. I could expel you of course."

Pinander flicks open the utility scroll on his belt and touches his bank account.

"So it's to be bribery?" Wigh smirks. "I think you're losing your grip."

"I'm a pragmatist."

"And that may be your undoing. To activate Lore, merely studying scrolls won't suffice, though it's essential."

"I just want to pass, Wigh."

"Then you're lost and the exam will catch you up. Nobody cheats the exam, even with insider tips. It's not just a test of knowledge. Otherwise we'd simply audit . . . what need of exams? Audit is passive. The exam requires your initiative and that's when things can get . . . emergent."

Cryptic doggerel, Professor Wigh's specialty. But this tidbit finds purchase in Pinander's activated mind and plants roots.

6

Raff shares a dorm room with seven other students, all home and embunked, muttering incantations, rocking obsessively back and forth, scribbling verse on walls, or unconscious. Pinander climbs onto Raff's bunk and finds her huddled in a nest of blinking, formatted scrolls. After staring a moment she recognizes her visitor.

"I hope you didn't come to express your condolences, Pinander. I can't handle one more condolence."

"Jain's in Detention."

Detention, aestivation, lost in a second dream-time, possibly indefinite. Pinander can't imagine where else they would put her now, and it's a kind of death.

"Sorry," Raff says, all her bluster deflated.

"And I'm sorry about Ivier. He seemed solid to me. Not the sort to fold under exam pressure."

"He wasn't." Raff frowns, studying her guest with realization. "What are you doing here? Shouldn't you be studying?"

"Just before they took her, she told me about Ivier's extracurricular reading?"

Raff's gaze darkens.

"Did you read it too?" Pinander says, glancing at Raff's mess of formatted scrolls.

"I was tempted. I wanted to understand what had done that to him . . . " She inhales, stifling a half-sob. "I couldn't take the plunge. He was always braver than me. And more curious about everything. Before it really messed him up, he was railing against the empire. He told me one line of this Sinecure . . . 'Extinguish the Emanation.' Real counterrevolutionary stuff."

"With Jain it was physics."

He's already thinking of her in the past tense. Philo and Ivier, and who knows who else, committed straightforward suicide because of their new knowledge, or dual mind or whatever it is, but Jain also killed herself, in a way.

"I'm happy to commiserate all you want. I'm completely fucked, exam-wise, so I'm done studying. But you . . . " She follows Pinander's gaze to the blinking scrolls. " . . . you really want to read it? What about your scholarship? You're on a full ride from . . . where was it?"

"Broken Pearl?"

"And didn't you just come out of audit? They know you know about Sinecure. If she's really such a dangerous revelation, why would they let you go?"

Maybe it was a faulty audit. Maybe they didn't find his love of Jain wanting. Maybe they didn't find it at all, and maybe they missed other things as well. Maybe he's dangerous.

"I didn't delete it," Raff says. "These scrolls were my study notes. I'm washing out, that's all. I didn't read Sinecure, but Ivier's distillations have scrambled me anyway. Even if I could stand singing another fucking

Ode, I wouldn't want to graduate from this place. I'll go home and my parents will resent me, and I'll be just another trust-funded wastrel until the whole system comes crashing down, or I'm rich. But I didn't delete it. I didn't read her, after all. What if she's as important as Ivier said? So, I just passed her along . . . to someone I thought could handle it."

7

Broken Pearl, in the Mother-of-Pearl system, is twenty lightyears away, but thanks to Emanation technology—some of which Pinander came to understand just hours ago—the conversation lag is nonexistent.

"We trust you're doing us proud, kid."

Da's seemingly benign catchphrase resonates with its usual menace. Cue Ma's more insidious addendum:

"You won't forget the sacrifices we made to get you there. We know that."

They look so old. In addition to the seven lost aestivation years, there had been dilation getting here from Broken Pearl.

"And the exam is . . . "

"In three days, Da. Like I said."

"Alright kid, check your tone."

"Go easy on him, darling, he's under pressure."

"Doesn't give him call to act high-handed with his own father."

"Sorry Da."

Their backdrop is the old familiar bulkhead, encrusted with archaeological layers of his childhood, video prints of Pinander, age zero to eleven. From twelve to the present there was no family life. They consigned him to aestivation without a second thought. In his darker moments, he thinks that was no better than selling him into prostitution or soldiery, but he can't afford to indulge such thinking.

"So what are your plans tonight?" Ma asks. A loaded question of course.

"Studying."

"Good lad," Da says.

Pinander takes a subversive delight in the lie. He really should study, but instead he's going to crash his first student party.

8

"Ethics are laws written on our hearts.

Laws are ethics written on space-time.
Never forget the beginner's mind."

It's verse ninety-five of the Ninth Epic, but shrieked over a decadent soundtrack that pulses through the compound. The revelers sway drunkenly, heads hanging, amid rolling storm-fronts of smart vapor. Here in the compounds this is possible, where obscene wealth keeps campus law at bay. Compared to these students, dorm denizens, still fabulously wealthy by empire standards, might as well be paupers.

Pinander wonders what that makes him.

Wandering through ornate gardens in his black student robe, he draws looks from fashionably and scantily clad partygoers. There is commotion ahead, a crowd psychedelically blurred by smart vapor. He gives it wide berth—a fight, from what he can hear. Someone stole someone's meds. This contributes to Pinander's sense of being an alien here. It is usually the most privileged students who engage in theft, violence, and drugs. He remembers Philo lobbing a cannister of vandalism nano at the façade of The Crypt. Pinander couldn't fathom this. Philo's clan paid a fortune to send him here, and he was an adult choosing to stay. And there were Jain's countless transgressions, up to and including her novel suicide.

He wonders if he can raise her from the dead.

"Our great dream is the Inevitable Peace.
Entangled colonies, instantaneous,
Civilization their inheritance."

Verse thirty-four of the Twentieth Temple Ode. Pinander recalls it activating a fine blend of dark energy and political theory. That was just a few weeks ago, but it seems like centuries. He marvels at how the ancients subtly weaved physical and social science, making them only actionable together. In the face of that sorcery, this setting of Odes to hedonist beats seems juvenile.

"Pinander, isn't it?"

The haze clears. He tried to hold his breath, but smart vapor must've gotten in.

Before him sits an antlered figure on a phantasmagoric throne, a heap of mutated idolatry printed for the occasion. This person seems to be holding court. A modded menagerie is arrayed on either side of the throne, students become mythic animal people, chimeras, and strange gods.

Pinander struggles to focus on their lord.

"You're that scholar-shipper Philo mentioned."

She wears a student robe artfully shredded to showcase her powerful—and no doubt expensive—musculature. The crystalline antlers erupting from her temples are not a mod, but the side effect of a perilous drug. Pinander can't remember the name of that particular moneyed pastime, but it strikes him as germane.

Something to do with why he's here.

"He called you a pragmatist. So not to be inhospitable, but why are you here?"

"Not winning the masque at any rate!"

This barb from a translucent, many-limbed demigod gets the menagerie giggling. Pinander becomes self-conscious. His head clears.

"That's enough, there will be decorum in the court. Pinander the Pragmatic, you are welcome here and shall enjoy my protection. I was sorry to hear about Jain and Philo."

"Thank you, Decima."

For it is she, Decima the Decimated, Queen of Campus Hedonists, consumer of more drugs and brain mods than anyone in university lore.

"If you seek safe harbor from the storm of thy grief, we of the happy hunting grounds can aid you."

Surrounded by her tittering followers, Decima locks gazes with Pinander. She seems bored with her pantomime. Pinander guesses his presence ruins the mood. In contact with anything beyond her world of privilege, the bubble of her legendary status threatens to burst. The menagerie quiets down.

The translucent demigod steps toward Pinander. "I don't think you were invited."

This one's eyes are yellow, and not from some reptilian mod. He twitches and glares, his varied arms spasming with potential.

"He's looking for this, I guess."

Decima holds up a scroll.

The demigod glares with keyed up paranoia. "What is it?"

"What I don't get is why Raff handed it to me. We're not particularly close."

"She thought . . . " Pinander hesitates. "Given your hobby? That is . . . "

"I see. My mind is already so expanded and abused, why couldn't I endure two Lore contexts at once?"

"It's the reputation you've cultivated."

She holds the scroll up to blood-red methane moonglow.

"Ours is the unremitting struggle,
The emperor-less empire,
The dynasty without a sire!"

Verse forty-six, growled pretentiously over the quickening beat. Pinander recalls the Lore it activated. He wonders if Sinecure has new contexts for accelerated expansion and manifest destiny.

"I guess you haven't read her yet?" he says.

"She was going to top off my evening."

"I've heard about it," the demigod says, his agitation mounting.

"And what have you heard? Please do enlighten the court."

"Just . . . that it could turn everything upside down."

"That doesn't intrigue you? Why do you think I convoked this court?"

"To expand our minds . . . "

"And Sinecure might be the ultimate psychedelic."

"She could tear down everything we have."

Smart vapor makes flickering palaces of the suites bordering the gardens. The stupefied menagerie watches their queen. She flicks open the scroll.

"Don't!"

A demigod arm lashes out, unrolling like a tentacle. Pinander stares in amazement. He had no idea the seemingly ornamental limb was that functional. He wonders how much it cost. At least the full value of his scholarship.

The tentacle withdraws and dangles the scroll over the demigod's head.

"Give it back." Decima rises from her throne.

"Forget everything else," the demigod says, "but I can't lose you."

Pinander finds himself in headlong motion, sprinting toward the translucent devil, even after he sees the scroll strobing, formatting. He knows it's too late but he's charging. Maybe he "has the vapors" as these elite students say. He's never felt this violent in his life.

Decima, rushing from the other direction, looks how he feels.

9

The statue in the Hall Paramount towers over rows of holding seats, all currently empty except for Decima and Pinander. They slouch beside each other in their constraints, bruised and groggy. Decima twitches and sweats with a variety of withdrawals.

"I can't believe this is happening," Pinander says, his voice low in this templelike space of The Crypt. He has failed Jain, Sinecure, his parents.

"Then it isn't happening," Decima says. "Nothing is, but belief makes it so."

"Elitist twaddle."

The statue, an imperial factor in flowing robes, glares down at them in judgment. Weald was a paragon of ancient officialdom: grave and cultured, fair-minded and sober, able to summon verse for any occasion. The curriculum council needed a model mind when designing their uploads. Now every sitter of the exam must strive to be Weald.

"Where's Gnomic?" Decima says.

"That fuckwit we beat to a pulp? In the infirmary I guess. You need a certain level of health to aestivate. You and I barely made the grade, I think."

This seems to increase her confusion. "Where are we?"

"The Crypt, mush-head! Slated for punitive aestivation!"

"But . . . "

"But you're rich and you live in the suites. But one of your own summoned campus police and let them in. Because a lowly scholarshipper laid hands on elite flesh, I guess."

"You shouldn't have done that."

"You shouldn't have spiked your vapor with . . . whatever that was."

Vault doors hiss open somewhere. Footsteps echo through the hall. This is it. He'll be joining Jain in perpetual twilight, not that he'll see her there. So much time already lost, now more. Maybe this time he won't wake up.

"Unbind her."

Two smartly suited people come around the statue, followed by a chastened-looking monk in gray habit. The monk hurries over to barely conscious Decima and incants to her seat in his crypt monk speech. The off-campus suits stare at Pinander impassively. He guesses they're functionaries of some kind from Decima's powerful clan, lawyers maybe, or glorified enforcers warranted to throw money around.

The chair releases Decima and the suits get her up. One of them puts an infuser to her neck. She twitches to life as they escort her away, and she glances back at him.

"I'm sorry."

10

The leaking, overcrowded estates hung from the ice ceiling of Broken Pearl's crust. The inky void of the interior sea yawned below, a living metaphor reminding denizens of their precarious economic position. Pinander spent his childhood harvesting exotic proteins from the water filters. It could be traded at the bazaars and processed into all manner of black-market commodities. Many of his fellow filter raiders—children all, only they could fit in the filters—succumbed to prion exposure, but somehow Pinander survived. Da took this for evidence of his son's special destiny. Da always thanked his abyssal gods that the Mother-of-Pearl system was entangled with the empire. He prayed for the empire at their home shrine. He prayed his son would sit the exam and become an Imperial Factor. Pinander never prayed, but he studied the shrine's myriad figurines. Among the abyssal gods were imperial figures, including a miniature Paragon Weald, more crudely represented than in The Crypt.

"Abyssal Lord." Da's eyes squeezed shut, voice low. "Queen of the Vents, Sireless, Paragon Weald, I petition for my only son . . . "

The gods seem to hear him. Pinander feels the universe subtly shift. He is no longer in Broken Pearl.

"Can you hear me?" A familiar voice in a radiant void.

"Yes . . . "

"You were aestivating."

His thoughts rally. "Yes."

"You're still in the casket, but I've quickened you into semiconsciousness."

He can feel the casket around him. "How long was I under?"

"A day."

"Who are you?"

"Your long-suffering professor."

"Wigh . . . what is this? Get me out of here!"

"I will, but I wanted to give you a choice first. Concerning Sinecure. You could still read her if you wish."

"The scroll got formatted. There's another? Explain yourself, Wigh. No more obfuscation!"

"There was good reason for that. I couldn't be specific, in case you got audited again."

"Ethics are laws written on our hearts.
Laws are ethics written on space-time.
Never forget the beginner's mind."

That verse activated much Lore. A core verse of Paragon Weald's own writing, it was foundational when his mind was modeled. One of the secrets it unlocked was the composition of the atmosphere held at bay by the university shield. This shield was an invisible mystery called a "spin foam hack." The lethal brew of the atmosphere was revealed to him:

nitrogen, methane, a dash of hydrogen, ethane, propane, cyanoacetylene, helium, argon, hydrogen cyanide . . .

"Pin!"

"Yes . . . "

"Stay with me. I can't wake you up completely or the casket's alarm gets triggered. I'm on the auditing council, at least for a bit longer. I've got you interfaced for audit right now."

"Wait, last time . . . "

"I got you released. I made sure I was your reviewer."

"Then I'm dangerous after all?"

"I think you can handle both contexts at once. I know I can't. It's not that I'm too old, but there's something to be said for an honest reckoning with yourself. The audits of my youth taught me that. I think you know what I mean."

He never stopped thinking of the toxic atmosphere hanging over him. It was denser than the breathable mix inside the university bubble. He imagined the shield straining under the weight. The students around him never seemed troubled by it, never looked up into the hazy fathoms. He broached this with Jain and Philo, and they mocked his lack of understanding, though theirs went no deeper.

What they really mocked was his lack of faith.

"You're interfaced, so I can link you to the Faculty Library."

Later he would come to understand the shield, the manipulation of space-time quanta, but this did not alleviate his sense of dread. With more verses came more activated Lore, more insights on space-time, the foundational science of the empire. It also meant space-time was the ultimate data storage medium. Nothing written on the Great Substrate could be erased. Here on campus, it was accessible only in the Faculty Library.

"The choice is yours," Wigh says.

"And if I choose knowledge, what do you expect to happen?"

"Based on what I saw in your audit . . . You survive the dual mind, you hold both contexts in your mind at once and become something new, a hybrid. You sit the exam and write essays that shake the empire. Or you go mad."

11

Ranging far over four-dimensional topographies of knowledge, through valleys of species profiles, steppelands of history, human and alien, you find piddling skeans of familiar Lore. Your imperial conditioning renders most novelties abstruse. All that is alien or remote appears threatening, unfathomable.

Paragon Weald was not the beacon of intellectual curiosity you've been sold.

You search desperately for the works of Sinecure. You spend subjective years searching. You grow old in this search, but eventually find her.

"Sun by sun,
The future comes undone."

With her first lines, a new, conflicting context for the Lore takes hold. Already Weald is no longer a paragon, but a venal, pretentious bureaucrat, a creature of vice and a status inheritor. And the empire itself, The Emanation . . .

"Pin!"

It's Wigh again, far away, across landscapes, with your physical body.

"Throw illusions in the fire.
Old men stare at glowing embers
As though at runes to be deciphered."

The empire is no longer a beacon of hope, but a metastasizing thing, alive and ravenous and amoral. No, it's both beacon and cancer, and Weald is both paragon and degenerate. Your mind threatens to split along these contradictions.

"Work with me Pin." She's dragging you across the aestivation deck. "Our escape window is short. Get up!"

Sinecure's new context is like a new language, forcing you to rethink the universe from a new lingual perspective. Sinecure's language dissects where Weald's embellishes. Sinecure is concise where Weald is purple. But you've already experienced this. You're remembering it, in a sense. You were interfaced with the Faculty Library and now you're not. The trauma of dual mind is still playing out in your skull, like a biome killer spewing nuclear winter years after impact.

"On your feet or we're not going to make it!"

You saw Sinecure herself from two perspectives. From her own, a member of the curriculum council secreting pieces of herself into the Weald-dominated model, for the greater good of the universe; and from Weald's, who branded her a counterrevolutionary.

"That's it."

You stumble along behind Wigh, shivering in your aestivation caul.

"This will be it for me," the professor whispers, "but that's okay. The least I can do really. I cultivated my cryptic demeanor for years, you know, in case someone like you or Jain came along. In case I had to talk around audits."

"They're going to get you," you say. "Even dead you'll be audited. So no matter what you've done in here, they'll be coming after me."

"Ever the pragmatist. That's right Pin."

"And how did a hard copy of Sinecure's work get onto campus in the first place?" It just occurred to you to ask her this.

Wigh runs to the edge of the hallway, muttering and gesturing her key cant at the door.

"Professor?"

Without turning to face him, she says, "Yes Pin, they're all on my head. Philo and Jain, all of them. Maybe you as well. Soon I'll be dead and audited, as you said, and they'll be after you. You've got to change everything before that happens. I gambled with lives and I'm going to pay for it, rest assured. You'll be sitting the exam in a few hours. I think I bought you that much time."

"All this for essays by me?"

Your two minds war within your skull. You want to report this murderous dissident. And you want to forgive her sins, or at least set them aside, and see her plan out to its logical conclusion.

"All for essays by you, and they'd better be good. They need to accomplish a paradigm shift."

12

"The big day!" Ma says.

Her tense grin is nearly a snarl. Your mother the slavish, brainwashed disciple of the empire who sacrificed her only son on its altar; your mother, a good citizen, someone who thinks for herself and chooses the empire, the Emanation, and the best possible life for her son.

"Are you prepared?" Da asks.

Your father, superstitious, blindly-laboring drone of a backwater colony, ignorant, unyielding, a monster; your father, paragon in his own right, the kind of man on whose back the empire rests.

Your cramped eight-bunk room is a prison cell, and a unique privilege.

"Pin? Are you okay?"

"Answer your mother, kid."

The ansible that connects you to them rests on quantized spacetime. That is true in both of your minds. But the upshot is not mere entanglement, not just colonization. "The physics kept me going," Jain once said. "The grand mystery of it all. She puts it in a new light." You focus on the majestic, entangled oneness of the cosmos when you feel your mind threatening to disintegrate.

"Am I okay? I'm not sure how to answer that, Ma."

"Did you get any sleep?" she asks, growing anxious.

"Of course not," Da says, "he's been studying all night. Haven't you, kid?"

True either way you look at it. You've spent the night digesting the perspective shift of Sinecure. You've had an empire-affirming collision with a counterrevolutionary. You don't see how it can be both. You lean forward on your elbows and clutch your skull. Your seven bunkmates are asleep.

"Do you have a headache?"

"More of a mind-ache." And you could make it go away. You could join those who went before you. It would be easy. You could use Philo's method, nice and quick.

"He's working hard. A little discomfort is to be expected. I'm proud of him." Da puts a hand on his wife's shoulder, a rare display of affection. "He'll be okay. The kid won't let us down. He knows what we've sacrificed to get him there."

"Yeah, me."

"Excuse me?"

"Me, Da. You sacrificed me."

"What the hell do you mean?"

Ma is sobbing.

"You'd better apologize, kid."

"Ma, Da . . . I'm sorry, but I think I'm a counterrevolutionary."

You snort, and the snort becomes a chuckle, then you're cackling, tears streaming, your cellmates rising from their bunks to grumble, and you can't stop.

13

In the amber predawn gloaming, the black-robed graduating class encircles a great bonfire at the center of campus. Each student is penning a verse of their choice—from the Odes or Epics or Songs—onto a ceremonial wooden tablet. Hooded professors wander the circle, peering over shoulders.

You dip your brush in the nearest brazier-well. Holding the tablet in your left hand, you apply the brush with your right:

"Ethics are laws written on our hearts," you murmur as you pen.

Other students murmur around you. You glance up and see Decima about one hundred and sixty degrees along the circle, nearly lost to view behind the fire. Her antlers have been shaved down to nubs. She is black robed like everyone else and staring back at you intently.

"Laws are ethics written on space-time," you pen.

Closer, Raff frowns and dabs clumsily at her tablet.

There is no sign of Wigh among the professors.

"Never forget the beginner's mind."

This was Weald's favorite verse. Sinecure despised its meaning and intent, but as a connoisseur of propaganda she admired its craft. You find it banal, but the calligraphy is simple. You feel a professor at your back, inspecting briefly then moving on.

Soon the professors have gathered closer to the fire, their backs to it, facing various quadrants of students.

"Embody the text," one of them says.

"Embody the text," others repeat.

You kneel with the other students in loose unison. You hold your tablet over a copper basin, angled forty-five degrees as instructed. You drop your ink-hemorrhaging brush in the basin. With your liberated right hand, you pick up a mug of water and pour it on the tablet. Your calligraphy blurs and runs.

The inky water collects in the basin.

Soon you're standing, basin held in both hands, like the other students.

"Embody the text," the professors say, this time in chorus.

This ritual's roots go far back in space-time, possibly to the origin world. Both Weald and Sinecure had a nostalgic fondness for it, a rare point of agreement between the ghosts in your head. You raise the basin to your lips and drink. The inky water is bitter, mildly nauseating, but you keep your composure. When everyone has drunk, the circle contracts, students approaching the fire with their blank tablets. You go with them, still of two minds, but alive, maintaining, not suicidal. For solace you have more than the entangled oneness of the cosmos. You have Jain. You have the idea of her, her ambition, and you can only save her by favoring one context over another.

You consign your tablet to the flames. It's time.

14

In your spartan examination cell, you slouch over the dedicated exam scroll and read the first essay prompt:

"Politically contrast the revolutionaries who launched the empire with the counterrevolutionaries who have been trying to tear it down for millennia, using Lore activated by verse thirty-three of Song Five, verse fifty-six of the Temple Odes, and verse twenty-one of the Paramount Epic."

You have most of that, and some has been redundantly activated by Sinecure. It's multifaceted, letting you see it like no one before you. You think for a moment, put stylus to scroll, and begin to write.

ABOUT THE AUTHOR

Andy Dudak is a writer and translator of science fiction. His original stories have appeared in *Analog, Apex, Clarkesworld, Daily Science Fiction, Interzone, The Magazine of Fantasy and Science Fiction,* Rich Horton's Year's Best, and elsewhere. He's translated twelve stories for *Clarkesworld,* and a novel by Liu Cixin, among other things. In his spare time he likes to binge-watch peak television and eat Hui Muslim style cold sesame noodles.

Ghosts of Christmas Past: The Victorian Christmas Ghost Story Tradition

CARRIE SESSAREGO

"Marley was dead, to begin with," says Charles Dickens in the most famous Christmas ghost story. While modern readers continue to enjoy *A Christmas Carol*, few are aware that it was one of hundreds of Christmas-themed ghost stories that flourished in written form during the Victorian era. These stories represented a perfect meeting of interest in science and in spiritualism, in the availability of cheap printed fiction, and in the acceptance in England of Christmas as a major holiday with customs we continue to practice today.

The tradition of telling ghost stories in the winter seems to be a very old one, referenced as far back as William Shakespeare's *A Winter's Tale*, and Christopher Marlowe's *The Jew of Malta*. As Jerome K. Jerome put it in 1891:

> *"Whenever five or six English-speaking people meet 'round a fire on Christmas Eve, they start telling each other ghost stories. Nothing satisfies us on Christmas Eve but to hear each other tell authentic anecdotes about specters. It is a genial, festive season, and we love to muse upon graves, and dead bodies, and murders, and blood."*

However, Christmas was considered a minor holiday in England and in America at the beginning of the Victorian era, which lasted from 1837—1901 (with the careers of many authors overlapping the beginning and end of the era somewhat). Christmas celebrations were banned by the Puritan Parliament of 1647 and throughout much of the

1700s Christmas was celebrated quietly, if at all. In the absence of other festivities, winter ghost stories persisted, according to Henry Bourne, who wrote in 1725 that "nothing is commoner in country places than for a whole family in a winter's evening to sit 'round the fire and tell stories of apparitions and ghosts."

Regency aristocrats, who loved any excuse to throw a party, celebrated "The Twelve Days of Christmas," with Christmas Day itself as a quiet day for family and church. They reserved the largest of the Twelve Day celebrations for January 6, the Feast of Epiphany. Regency aristocrats and gentry decorated with winter greenery, and over the course of the twelve days they enjoyed a Yule log, games, dancing, and mummery. Gift giving was minimal, and there were no Christmas trees or visits from Santa. A genteel family, such as those featured in Jane Austen's *Emma*, saw the season as a sensible excuse for family visits, a dinner, and possibly a dance. As Mr. Elton observes,

> *This is quite the season indeed for friendly meetings. At Christmas everybody invites their friends about them, and people think little of even the worst weather.*

Christmas Day was not even a day off for most people, as it was not recognized as a Bank Holiday in the UK until 1871, which is why Bob Cratchit, in 1843's *A Christmas Carol*, enjoys a modest feast with his family on Christmas Eve but must hurry to work on Christmas Day.

The combined forces of Queen Victoria and Charles Dickens led to the opulent Christmas celebrations that we see today. Queen Victoria was charmed by Prince Albert's description of a German Christmas tree, and made the custom of having a decorated tree common in England. She emphasized Christmas as a family time that included, and indeed centered, children. Gift giving became popular, and an inexpensive postal service led to the practice of sending Christmas Cards. Father Christmas, formerly a feature of adult celebrations, gradually became interchangeable with the American Santa Claus and delivered presents to good boys and girls, in accordance with his description in "A Visit from Saint Nicholas" by Clement Clarke Moore (written in 1823). Authors and artists such as Charles Dickens, Washington Irving, and Thomas Nast spread the word and popularized these new features of Christmas.

Into this atmosphere came cheap printed material—and an abundance of Christmas-themed stories for popular consumption. At this time, literacy was so sufficiently widespread that most illiterate people could find someone to read out loud for them. This was a common entertainment not only at home, but also in public houses. The 1830's saw the advent of inexpensive serialized fiction that kept printed matter affordable and addictive as literacy continued to spread thanks to educational reforms. The tradition of telling stories at winter crystallized into a new written phenomenon.

Many periodicals sold annual collections, specially bound and suitable for gift giving, as well as special editions of Christmas stories. Charles Dickens published a weekly literary magazine called *Household Words*, followed by another magazine, *All the Year Round*. Both had extra Christmas issues for which Dickens and other authors wrote Christmas stories. The 1863 Christmas issue offered seven stories for fourpence (in today's money, about $1.78 US dollars). Several other periodicals followed a similar practice, thus converting an oral tradition into a new written one.

This loose definition led to an amazing variety of stories, from the terrifying to the comical to the gruesome to the heartwarming. Mary Oliphant uses her sweet and touching story "The Lady's Walk" to explore the economic and social pressures on a young woman in rural Scotland. Jerome K. Jerome's story "The Ghost of the Blue Chamber" is hilariously funny. Louisa May Alcott's novella *The Abbot's Ghost; Or, Maurice Treherne's Temptation*, originally published under the name A.M. Barnard, is a romance. "How Peter Parley Laid a Ghost," an anonymous story in a children's publication, strives to be entertaining and educational, and teaches children not to be afraid of ghosts, not even ones like the rumored:

> *. . . implacable figure of a White Lady, who sat on the keystone of the arch, engaged in the doleful, but tidy duty of combing her long golden hair, for the better accomplishment of which occupation the lady carried her head in her lap.*

The Victorian era was one of intense tension between public fascination with science and with spiritualism, a tension that only added to the popularity of printed ghost stories and influenced their content. Charles Darwin's theory of evolution upended science, religion, and philosophy. Naturalists, both professional and amateur, collected and studied plant and animal species across the globe. Explorers mapped the poles and astronomers mapped the skies. Arthur Conan Doyle's Sherlock Holmes made his first appearance in "A Study in Scarlet," which was printed in Beeton's Christmas Annual. The Sherlock Holmes stories emphasized rational, calm, logical deduction over superstition and intuition. Anything seemed possible.

In keeping with this scientific age, many Victorian Christmas ghost stories sought to explain the seemingly supernatural phenomenon by mundane means at the end of the story. This sometimes had a preachy tone, as if to say, "How silly must one be to believe in ghosts!" Dickens makes especially hilarious fun of spiritualists in "The Haunted House," in which an unfortunate man must share a train compartment with a spiritualist:

> *"You will excuse me," said the gentleman contemptuously, "if I am too much in advance of common humanity to trouble myself at all about it. I have passed the night—as indeed I pass the whole of my time now—in spiritual intercourse.""O!" said I, something snappishly.*

The gentleman goes on to relate the spirit's most recent communications:

> *"A bird in the hand," said the gentleman, reading his last entry with great solemnity, "Is worth two in the Bosh.""Truly I am of the same opinion," said I; "but shouldn't it be Bush?""It came to me, Bosh," returned the gentleman.*

The practice of spiritualism boomed during the Victorian era. Spiritualists believed that through a variety of means, mediums could facilitate communication between the living and the dead. They saw this as both a religious movement (one that championed abolition as well as rights for women) and as an extension of scientific experimentation. The very speed at which scientific discoveries and technological innovations were being made only added to the idea that a barrier between the living and the dead might quite plausibly and rationally be breached. In the words of historian Nicola Bown:

> *The Victorians were haunted by the supernatural. They delighted in ghost stories and fairy tales, and in legends of strange gods, demons, and spirits; in pantomimes and extravaganzas full of supernatural machinery; in gothic yarns of reanimated corpses and vampires. Even avowedly realist novels were full of dreams, premonitions, and second sight. It was not simply a matter of stories and storytelling, though, for the material world they inhabited often seemed somehow supernatural. Disembodied voices over the telephone, the superhuman speed of the railway, near-instantaneous communication through telegraph wires: the collapsing of time and*

distance by modern technologies that were transforming daily life was often felt to be uncanny.

In contrast to ghost stories that took great pains to establish mundane explanations, other stories were unabashedly and completely supernatural, in keeping not only with the fascination with spiritualism, specifically, but also with a general public fascination with death and with the unknown. These stories feature a wide variety of ghostly figures and creepy hallways, escaped lunatics and convicts, and musical instruments that play themselves.

More impressively, authors managed to wring chills from such mundane objects as a door knocker (*A Christmas Carol*, by Charles Dickens), bedsheets ("Oh, Whistle, and I'll Come to You, My Lad," by M. R. James), and a duffel bag ("The Kit-Bag," by Algernon Blackwood). "The Nutcracker and the Mouse King," by E. T. A. Hoffmann, naturally, wreaks terror with a cursed nutcracker and murderous mice, and "The Doll's Ghost," by F. Marion Crawford, involves a doll that says "Pa-pa." Famous ghost story author M. R. James offered this advice on writing ghost stories:

Many common objects may be made the vehicles of retribution, and where retribution is not called for, of malice. Be careful how you handle the packet you pick up in the carriage-drive, particularly if it contains nail-parings and hair. Do not, in any case, bring it into the house. It may not be alone . . .

A Christmas Carol is by far the most famous Christmas ghost story. Published in 1843, it was an instant hit. Dickens gave public readings of the story in England and America for years, giving at least one hundred and twenty-seven performances. Dickens' primary motivation, besides earning money for himself, was to spread awareness of the plight of the urban poor, and his book emphasized the idea of charitable giving at Christmas. It also popularized the new customs that Queen Victoria had introduced and created new ones. The book popularized the greeting, "Merry Christmas," and the saying, "Bah! Humbug," and demonstrated to readers that previously rural Christmas traditions could be incorporated into urban life. The book is also replete with ghosts, far many more than the Ghosts of Past, Present, and Future:

The air was filled with phantoms, wandering hither and thither in restless haste, and moaning as they went. Every one of them wore chains like Marley's Ghost; some few (they might be guilty governments) were linked together; none were free. Many had been personally known to Scrooge in their lives. He had been quite familiar with one old ghost, in a white waistcoat, with a monstrous iron safe attached to its ankle, who cried piteously at being unable to assist a wretched woman with an infant, whom it saw below upon a doorstep. The misery with them all was, clearly, that they sought to interfere, for good, in human matters, and had lost the power forever."

And the story is sometimes funny and sometimes touching, but often truly terrifying, as in this quote from earlier in the book:

After several turns, he sat down again. As he threw his head back in the chair, his glance happened to rest upon a bell, a disused bell, that hung in the room, and communicated for some purpose now forgotten with a chamber in the highest story of the building. It was with great astonishment, and with a strange, inexplicable dread, that as he looked, he saw this bell begin to swing. It swung so softly in the outset that it scarcely made a sound; but soon it rang out loudly, and so did every bell in the house. This might have lasted half a minute, or a minute, but it seemed an hour. The bells ceased as they had begun, together. They were succeeded by a clanking noise, deep down below; as if some person were dragging a heavy chain over the casks in the wine-merchant's cellar. Scrooge then remembered to have heard that ghosts in haunted houses were described as dragging chains. The cellar door flew open with a booming sound, and then he heard the noise much louder, on the floors below; then coming up the stairs; then coming straight towards his door.

While *A Christmas Carol* is the best-remembered Christmas story, it was preceded and followed by dozens of others. The definition of a "Christmas ghost story" is and was a loose one. In some stories, such as "Old Hooker's Ghost; or, Christmas Gambols at Huntingfield Hall," Christmas celebrations are woven directly into the story and are integral to the plot. Other stories barely refer to the holiday but are still considered Christmas stories. M. R. James' "Oh, Whistle, and I'll Come to You, My Lad" never directly references Christmas, but takes place during a professor's winter holiday and thus earns a lasting place in "Best Christmas Ghost Story" lists. Henry James' "The Turn of the Screw" uses a framing device that takes place at Christmas, beginning,

> *The story had held us, 'round the fire, sufficiently breathless, but except the obvious remark that it was gruesome, as, on Christmas Eve in an old house, a strange tale should essentially be, I remember no comment uttered 'til somebody happened to say that it was the only case he had met in which such a visitation had fallen on a child.*

While the Victorians achieved a peak level of Christmas ghost stories in written form, the phenomena of telling spooky stories in the winter season in general, and on Christmas Eve specially, preceded the era and lives on in modified form today. Now, no Christmas holiday season is complete without a winter-themed horror novel or a new Christmas-themed horror movie. These movies are modern penny dreadfuls, often shot with a small or medium budget and consumed at home for a relatively small price. It seems that the urge to stay inside, get warm, and enjoy being scared in a safe environment endures.

ABOUT THE AUTHOR

Carrie Sessarego is the resident "geek reviewer" for *Smart Bitches, Trashy Books,* where she wrangles science fiction, fantasy romance, comics, movies, and non-fiction. Carrie's first book, *Pride, Prejudice, and Popcorn: TV and Film Adaptations of Pride and Prejudice, Wuthering Heights, and Jane Eyre,* was released in 2014. Her work has been published in *Interfictions Online, Pop Matters: After the Avengers, The WisCon Chronicles Vol. 9, Invisible 3, Clarkesworld Magazine,* and two volumes of *Speculative Fiction: The Year's Best Online Reviews, Essays and Commentary.* She spends her time wrangling her husband, daughter, dog, and three cats.

Hard Points of View: A Conversation with Stina Leicht

ARLEY SORG

When Stina Leicht was small, she wanted to grow up to be like Vincent Price—or so her website says. Instead, she grew up to be a writer who has impressed fans and critics alike.

Stina Leicht ("Pronounced 'Steena.' Think of it as Tina with an extra-added S. My last name is pronounced 'Lite,' like the beer.") was born in St. Louis, MO. She went to Sam Houston State University and the University of Houston; and studied 3D animation at Austin Community College. Leicht has worked as a bookseller, a graphic designer, and in the gaming industry. She has been a full-time writer and freelancer since 2005.

Leicht's debut novel, *Of Blood and Honey*, came out in 2011 with Night Shade Books, to strong reviews and acclaim, including landing as a finalist for the Crawford Award for best first fantasy. A historical fantasy set during the Troubles in 1970s Northern Ireland, it was followed by sequel *And Blue Skies from Pain* in 2012—fans placed Leicht on the finalist list for the Astounding Award (then called the Campbell Best New Writer award) in both 2012 and 2013.

In 2015 and 2017 Leicht published The Malorum Gates duology with Saga Press: *Cold Iron* and *Blackthorne*, books that received praise from venues such as *NPR* and Barnes & Noble; the latter book appeared on the Locus Recommended Reading list.

Her forthcoming title is "an enjoyable and thrilling read" according to *Library Journal*; *Persephone Station*, due from Saga Press in January of 2021.

Stina Leicht lives in central Texas. During the pandemic, she has been working on the next book and a few short stories. After more than a decade of not doing anything with her animation and graphic design skills, she has made a recent return to art, saying, "My mother and I started painting together over Zoom. It's pretty great." She plays Rock Band with husband Dane Caruthers. "My instrument of choice is the drums. I'm taking French lessons too. (Even if I'm dyslexic, go figure.)"

What was breaking in for you, how did it happen? Were there struggles or has it been a fairly easy journey?

Is anyone's journey easy? I doubt it. Although honestly, my story is kind of weird.

I've wanted to be a writer since I was in the seventh grade. However, my father actively discouraged me. So, I stopped writing.

In 2001, I was working as a well-paid graphic designer. However, the dot com bust happened and I was laid off on the day of my wedding. Not being able to find another graphic design job forced me to rethink my career. The only work available was minimum wage retail or coffee shop gigs. I decided on a bookstore. If nothing else, it was indirectly related to publishing and sounded fun. Going from making a substantial salary to less than minimum wage was depressing to say the least. Two months later, I found out I had breast cancer. It was at that point I decided it was time to start writing with the intent of becoming a professional. Why not? What was left to lose? (I'm totally fine now. Hurray for modern medicine!) Ultimately, writing was what kept me sane.

Also, I married well in the sense that my husband is amazing. We've been through so much together and we're still going strong. Anyway . . .

The bookstore (BookPeople) proved to be exactly the right place for me to be. I learned a lot about the publishing process. I practiced elevator pitches all day long (hand selling books), spoke with book reps, and met famous authors and sometimes their agents—Jeff VanderMeer, Holly Black, Neil Gaiman, Anne Rice, and Jasper Fforde to name a few. I also attended SlugTribe meetings (a local free writers' group for newbies) and signed up for ArmadilloCon's Writers' Workshop.

Then my husband was laid off. Financially, life totally sucked. We were so broke. But we had one another and I stayed focused on writing. During the second Writers' Workshop the guest editor, Jim Minz, liked my story so much he asked for my novel. While that was amazing, in the end he rejected it. (He was right to do so.) I learned how to bounce back from rejection. A very useful skill!

In 2009 Jeff VanderMeer asked me to contribute to *Last Drink Bird Head*. Amazingly, he took the story. That was my first big break. That same year I finished *Of Blood and Honey* and asked Holly for agenting advice. (She's such a kind and patient person.) She introduced me to Joe Monti. When Joe read my *OB&H* draft, he asked for some major changes. (I threw away 66,000 words of that first draft.) By the end of the year Joe became my agent. He sold my first novel to Night Shade Books that December.

I worked very hard to become the best writer I could. I studied. I read. I took classes. I listened to anyone who would speak to me about publishing. (I still do all these things.) Money was a struggle the whole way. At the same time, I've also been extremely lucky—as long as I've focused on writing. No other job situation worked out. That's what's weird. It's like the Universe stepped in and said, "Enough of that. Time to write."

On your site you describe Persephone Station as a "feminist SF novel." Were you always writing feminist works, even back in seventh grade when you were putting down words for your first novel? Or was there a process of shifting into feminist writing?

Interestingly enough, that first novel did have some feminist ideas. Mind you, they weren't well thought out, and I wasn't aware of what I was doing. I also wasn't a feminist, let alone an intersectional one. And that's why my first novels are mainly about straight white cis men. I'd absorbed the ridiculous idea that stories about other genders just weren't

Important. I wanted to be taken seriously. Internalized misogyny is such a bitch. I suppose a lot of women have this problem. Like Madge in the Palmolive commercials, we're all soaking in it.

That's why writing female point of view characters is *hard* for me. It took years to understand that not writing women was an issue. Joe wouldn't stop asking why, bless him. So, I relented. I eased into it with *Cold Iron* and *Blackthorne*.

At the exact same time, I raged about films that lacked women as characters. Some didn't even have women *in the background*. When women are portrayed, often they're minor, non-plot-affecting characters, or they're the love interest who gets killed off before the next movie. That's another thing that bugs me. Have you noticed how often women in films sleep with their male coworkers? It's rarer for them *not* to in movies and on TV. That's so not reality.

I didn't see how hypocritical it was to complain of stories not containing women and not writing stories about women. I bring this up because I feel it's important to learn, change, and grow. I've made some terrible mistakes. Everyone does. It's important to own them, though. You can't learn from mistakes you don't own. Hell, I wasn't even an intersectional feminist until around 2006. I learned. I continue to learn. I also continue to make mistakes, but I also improve as a person. I wish more Americans were okay with changing their minds. Being able to learn, apologize, and change our behavior is a positive trait.

One last thing: if no one demands to know the worldbuilding reason why there are no women in a story or film, then frankly no one needs a worldbuilding reason for why there are no men. For the record, there *are* men in *Persephone Station*. They're in the background. Some even have a line or two of dialogue.

Some even sleep with their coworkers.

How do you personally define space opera, what is the appeal of space opera to you, and what do you think is the appeal to readers?

For me, space opera is the fun stuff. It's *Star Trek* and *Star Wars*. It's a band of intergalactic criminals stuck on a living starship, having to learn how to cooperate in order to survive. The emphasis is adventure and interesting characters set against a vast backdrop. Actual science is a bonus. In the case of *Persephone Station*, most of that science is in the artificial intelligence aspects of the story. I do like to put something factual in my work. It's also good to encourage readers to think for themselves.

That said, I think escapism is what readers are looking for. They want Fun with a capital F—particularly now. It isn't fair that straight white cis men get all the stories. So, I'm writing for the rest of us.

There have been discussions in the field lately around "comps" (comparative descriptions of one work to other works), with many authors saying the comps assigned to their books by publicity teams weren't accurate. Persephone Station comps are The Mandalorian and Cowboy Bebop—do you feel like these are accurate? What are the important similarities between your book and those shows? Or are there better comps to draw on—and why?

The Mandalorian is a spaghetti western plus *Lone Wolf and Cub* set in space. I've only ever seen a few episodes of *Cowboy Bebop*, but it's an ensemble cast, and it too is influenced by Westerns. So, I think they're both good choices.

As you know, literature has a long history of riffing off of other genres. If you read Heinlein, Norton, Bradbury—any of the early "Golden Age SF" canon—you'll see the Western genre influence. *Firefly* wasn't the first, not even close. Even Gene Roddenberry pitched *Star Trek* to the TV executives as "a wagon train to the stars." Just listen to the opening: *Space: the final frontier*... I'm not even the first to take a Western genre film and transpose its plot into SF. Have you seen *Outland*? It's brilliant! The scriptwriters set *High Noon* in a space mining colony. Sean Connery plays the sheriff. I highly recommend it. Doctor Lazarus is one of my favorite female characters in a SF film.

You received a lot of recognition from your debut series, Fey and the Fallen: nominations two years in a row for the Astounding Award and short-listed for the IAFA William L. Crawford Fantasy Award. What, for you, was the impact of that attention?

I'm so grateful that happened. It was every bit as amazing as you'd imagine and extremely stressful at exactly the same time. I went from being a total unknown to having George R. R. Martin mispronounce my name on an international stage. The imposter syndrome was awful—particularly since the book I *thought* I'd written wasn't serious. (How hilarious is that?) I didn't see myself as a literary writer at all. I had it in my head that literary writers had degrees in literature. I definitely don't. It was confusing. There was so much pressure to write something new that did as well as that first novel. Oh my god, the sophomore slump is no joke. Poor Joe. He had to put up with me crying all over the front of his shirt. He really is the best. I'm so very lucky to have him in my work life. He gets my work. He's incredible—really one of my favorite people.

Are there important similarities and differences in your approach to narrative, structure, or other elements, between that first series and Persephone Station? Has your writing changed in significant ways?

As an artist, I was trained to paint in different styles. Having range as a writer is a good thing, I think.

With *Of Blood and Honey* I was obsessed with replicating a Northern Irish voice. So, I read a number of northern Irish crime writers' works. Some, like Adrian McKinty's, I read and reread so I could get the rhythm of the prose right. I allowed myself a certain flowery-ness in my language. It's expected in fantasy because fantasy, specifically urban fantasy, is more surreal, more dreamlike.

Fear was also a big part of how I wrote those books too. I was terrified of getting it wrong. I honestly didn't want to cause more harm. But I could only get so much information on The Troubles here in the US and most of that is written from . . . let's just say a decidedly *not* Catholic Nationalist perspective. The situation isn't much different from listening to a Trump supporter's version of events at a BLM march. I'm not saying that The Troubles is a Good vs. Evil dichotomy. Far from it. It was a civil war and human beings were involved. Humans are complicated beasties. At the same time, the victors definitely write history. That made research tricky. I also had to rely upon old photographs—black and white news photographs even—because I couldn't afford to go to Ireland. I was working at the bookstore for less than minimum wage, after all. So, I interviewed people who lived through it and that helped a lot. I spent so much time at the Ulster University CAIN website (cain.ulster.ac.uk). But there were holes in my research. There always will be in situations like that. Finding firsthand accounts of certain events was almost impossible to find. Life in The Maze prison for example. Unionists don't want to remember things like that. They erase it. (Or in the case of The Maze, bulldoze it.) Nonetheless, thanks to Ian MacDonald and Brian Magee, my friends in West Belfast, I was able to find most of what I needed. It still felt spotty. So, the plot jumps to different moments that I'm comfortable telling—kind of like stop-motion. It had the added advantage of replicating certain aspects of repeated trauma upon a victim's memory.

Persephone Station was its own adventure. I feel science fiction requires more direct language. It's an entirely different animal and the prose has to reflect that. So, I kept my prose as clean as possible. The action is punchy and over the top. The car chases are dog fights. The dialogue is quippy.

Overall, I like to think I've become a better writer. I've certainly learned more about writing than I ever thought I would. And yet, there's so much more to learn. Isn't that wonderful?

Back to the idea of Persephone Station as a "feminist SF novel." Why is the "feminist" distinction still important, and what does it mean specifically in terms of this work?

I'm a *Star Trek* fan. I definitely want to live in that future. If we are to create a world based upon equality, we must imagine it first. Diverse characters—all genders, all races need representation. Such casts reflect reality. But if that isn't enough to underscore the importance of diversity, studies have proven that reading helps people develop empathy. If there's one thing we need more of right now, it's empathy for people who aren't exactly like us. It's the only way humanity can save itself from destruction.

Everyone deserves a future.

For the record, when I use the word women I mean for it to include trans women. Trans women are women. Period.

Anyway, science fiction has a reputation as being written only by white cis men for white cis men. In my experience, readers don't much care for surprises. So, for *Persephone Station*, the feminist distinction is important. The novel is not only female-focused, its metaphors are femme-oriented as well. The weather reflects the feeling of a world that is hostile to the characters simply for being. The aliens display typical feminine qualities. They're invisible except when they have something those in power want. They're passive. They're diplomatic. They're groomed to conform to another's expectations to the extent that they become different people than who they really are. There's a lot of thought put into it.

Several reviews talk about this book as being fast paced. Craft-wise, what is the key to writing a fast-paced novel?

A tight outline is vital. I'm saying this, and I'm an organic writer. Ironic or what? In short stories, your words must serve multiple purposes due to limited space. The same is true for fast-paced novels. Don't waste words.

I tend to build upon the characters and setting at the start. Readers need to know when and where they are as soon as possible. (Unless it's your intent for the reader to feel lost.) Give readers hooky characters. This is key, in my opinion. It does no good to write punchy action if no one cares who the action is happening to. The scene will feel intense and fast if the reader is emotionally invested.

Lastly, movies aren't novels. It's important to know how many details are too much. I prefer to keep the prose short and punchy for action scenes. Get to the point. Use juicy adjectives. Remember the human brain can only track a certain amount of information in an emergency—and fights certainly count as emergencies. Some things will slip and that's okay. Remember that brains behave differently on adrenaline. So does the body. I recommend reading about the science of perception. The human brain is weird.

Is there anything else you really want readers to know about the book, beyond the blurbs and the reviews? What is special about this one for you?

We need more stories about women working together in groups, being smart, being friends, doing things that require courage and strength. I'm not talking about the Strong Woman trope. Women need to be people in stories, not a cis man's ideal of what a woman should be. We almost never see other genders in these relationships and situations—only straight cis men. I mean, romance is fine. I have a wonderful partner that I love. I get it. But there's more to life than being in a romantic relationship. Other genders need to see themselves living those options too. Also? Enough with the "There can be only one [fill in the blank non-cis white male]." routine already. That's why I wrote this book.

What was the most challenging aspect of writing this book, and how did you deal with the challenge?

For a start, I had to overcome my fear of writing SF. All my life I've heard about how women don't write science fiction. I've always secretly wanted to, but it's understood that fantasy is where women belong—particularly YA and urban fantasy. That's total bullshit, but it's the truth. I have this thing about "authorities" telling me that I can't do something. Mind you, it took a while to change gears, but I did it. I focused on the science that interested me—artificial intelligence, biology, and psychology. It's what male authors do. Why couldn't I?

Writing seven female characters, several of them as point of view characters, was a challenge too. To make it easier on myself, I took several of my favorite male characters and borrowed certain qualities from them. Then I approached the crew as women. What sorts of traditionally femme things do they like? What do *I* like? And it took off from there. I suspect that's why they're each such distinct people. What's the saying? Make your weaknesses your strengths?

You also have a Patreon. Is Patreon a good model for authors, is it the future of publishing? Or is it a platform some will find hard to utilize to significant effect?

I'm leery whenever anyone uses the expression "the future of publishing" in reference to anything electronic. If the computer age has proven one thing, it's its own impermanence. I can't tell you how many files I've lost over time because they're stored on Jazz drives or floppies or whatever software program that's no longer in use. The computer industry, in its race to programmed obsolescence (because PROFIT), has neglected to maintain its past. I could go on, but I won't.

Yeah. Yeah. I'm a GenX cynic.

Back to the subject, I do think Patreon is a great platform for artists. Just less so for writers. As with anything, there's no one solution for everyone. A lot of it depends upon how much you put into it. Also, Patreon doesn't tell you that you need to be already established. Building from scratch is extremely difficult.

For myself, I wasn't actually sold. I'm still not, not really. But I was tired of putting so much work into my blog for nothing. Sure, Feminist Monday is important work. The idea was that people—mainly male people—never saw the bigger picture. They'd maybe read one article and think that was all there was to that issue and move on, but feminism is more complex. It affects *everyone everywhere,* yes, even men. As my audience grew, I began to see results. Men wrote me to say they'd never thought about this or that aspect of our culture that way before. If you want a real mind bender, read *Invisible Women* by Caroline Criado Perez.

Sorry. Once a bookseller, always a bookseller.

Anyway, it was so much work. I got tired. K. Tempest Bradford talked me into starting a Patreon. It's not much, but it pays for itself as well as my website. That's enough for me. Of course, if I didn't have an extremely supportive partner, my priorities would be different. Naturally.

You have over a hundred posts on your Patreon. What can readers and fans look forward to if they become patrons?

I still do feminist posts, but not as often. Politics these days are so exhausting. I tend to post my artwork, talk about any new stories that get published, and discuss tarot cards. During October, I recommended horror comedies and matched them with songs.

What else are you working on, what else do you have coming up that you'd like readers to know about?

I'm working on a new space opera called *Loki's Ring*. It's another group of women working together—only this time they're an emergency response team. I've also got a story in *Evil in Technicolor*, a Horror anthology edited by Joe McDermott. And I wrote a humorous short story for my friend Martin Wagner for his BookTube channel.

ABOUT THE AUTHOR

Arley Sorg is co-Editor-in-Chief at *Fantasy Magazine*. A 2014 Odyssey Writing Workshop graduate, he writes SF/F/H, reviews for *Cascadia Subduction Zone Magazine*, and is also associate editor at both *Locus* and *Lightspeed* magazines.

Marvels and Horrors: A Conversation with Tim Pratt

ARLEY SORG

Long before winning a Hugo and a Rhysling, Tim Pratt worked as an advertising copywriter (briefly), and as a tech writer and office manager for a disability advocacy company. In 2001 he moved to Oakland, CA and landed a job as editorial assistant at *Locus Magazine*.

Born in Goldsboro, NC, as a child Pratt traveled with his mother, living in Missouri, Texas, Louisiana, and West Virginia, then back to Goldsboro. He graduated from Appalachian State University in Boone, NC with a BA in English, and then attended the Clarion Writers' Workshop in 1999.

That same year, Tim Pratt's stories started showing up: "53rd Annual Mantis Homecoming Dance" in *Maelstrom*, and "Angel of the Ordinary" in *Drabblecast*. In 2000 he had the poem "Visions" in *Star*Line*; plus more short fiction publications, including "The Fallen and the Muse of the Street" in *Strange Horizons*. Once his writing career had started, Pratt never stopped; instead, he cranked into high gear, continually putting out fiction (usually multiple pieces every year) and poetry.

By 2002, Pratt was appearing in readers' polls and earning major awards nominations. To date, he has appeared on ballots and short lists for the Sturgeon, Stoker, Nebula, World Fantasy, and much more. "Soul Searching," a poem published in *Strange Horizons* in 2004, won a Rhysling Award, and short story "Impossible Dreams" in the July 2006 *Asimov's* won their Readers' Poll and earned Pratt a Hugo Award for Best Short Story.

Meanwhile, Pratt also edited *Star*Line* from 2002 to 2004 and coedited *Flytrap* with his wife Heather Shaw from 2003—2008. He also edited reprint anthology, *Sympathy for the Devil*, and coedited original anthology *Rags and Bones* with Melissa Marr.

For most folks, this would be more than enough to keep them busy. But Pratt's "high gear" is a world apart. Already an accomplished and prolific short story author and poet, as well as a respected editor, in 2005 Pratt came out with debut novel, *The Strange Adventures of Rangergirl*, with Bantam Spectra. His first novel was a Mythopoeic Award finalist and won the Emperor Norton Award for best Bay area novel.

As T.A. Pratt, his urban fantasy series with "ass-kicking sorcerer" Marla Mason hit shelves in 2007, beginning with *Blood Engines*. In 2010 he had science fantasy *The Nex*; he had contemporary fantasy *Briarpatch* in 2011; and "gonzo historical" *The Constantine Affliction* in 2012—written under the name T. Aaron Payton; plus novella *The Deep Woods* with PS Publishing in 2014. He has also written gaming tie-ins for Forgotten Realms, Pathfinder Tales, and more.

Tim Pratt has authored over twenty novels, including a dozen books in the Marla Mason series, the more recent Axiom space opera trilogy (*The Wrong Stars*, *The Dreaming Stars*, and 2019's *The Forbidden Stars*, published by Angry Robot), plus several collections, including his latest, *Miracles & Marvels*.

He writes a new story every month for patrons at *www.patreon.com/timpratt* and continues to sell short fiction professionally. His newest book is *The Fractured Void*, a media tie-in for the Twilight Imperium game. His upcoming novel is *Doors of Sleep*, due from Angry Robot in January of 2021. Tim Pratt lives and writes buckets and buckets of words in Berkeley, CA, with his wife and their son, River. He even occasionally collaborates with family, saying, "My son and I designed a fun fast science fiction card game, and are in the process of making it pretty (had to commission a lot of art)."

If ISFDB is to be believed, your first stories came out in 1999. Not only do you have an incredible amount of work out, but you have so many different kinds of work, spanning two decades. You also have upcoming books with various publishers, plus your short story exclusives on Patreon. What does it take to stay in the game for so long and to sustain a career?

It's true! My first story was a nasty little piece of horror in a stapled 'zine called *Maelstrom SF*, edited by Dave Felts. From small acorns grow modestly sized oaks, etc.

As for the secret to my longevity, I just . . . like writing. I always wrote a lot. I started writing fiction steadily when I was in second or third grade and just never stopped. If all the markets suddenly stopped buying my work, I would still write it. (I would admittedly revise a lot less, and as for proofreading, pfft, never again.) If I didn't enjoy writing, I would stop; take away the element of fun and challenge and experimentation, and frankly, there are other endeavors with a higher ratio of return to effort. Written fiction is just my favorite art form. Certainly, there are aspects of the profession I find less fun or interesting or rewarding, but it's worth doing them to get all the parts I *do* like.

On a professional level, there are two other crucial elements for longevity, which I'd call "don't be precious" and "try stuff." I debuted pretty strong, sold five books to Bantam in like a year and a half or something, and then publishing had its great collapse in 2008 and I was suddenly out of contract and couldn't sell to a major publisher. Other people in that position quit writing, or quit doing it professionally. But I decided I shouldn't be precious. I took on interesting work-for-hire gigs that would teach me things instead; how to write for kids, how to write sword-and-sorcery, how to write satire, etc. For original work, I went to the small press. My feeling is, if you can't sell out arenas anymore, there's no shame in playing small clubs for your devoted fans.

Being willing to innovate went right along with that. If I'd kept getting good advances from major publishers, I wouldn't have experimented so much, but I explored crowdfunding and self-publishing with great success. I did the Patreon thing so I could focus on stories more. I edited anthologies. I expanded my sense of what my career could be. When urban fantasy was waning commercially, I thought, that's fine; I like doing other stuff, too. I like space opera, so I wrote some space opera, and my career had a nice little renaissance. Don't be precious. If something isn't working, try something else. Play for the love of the game.

You moved around quite a bit as a kid. And now you have Doors of Sleep coming up, where Zax is constantly on the move, against his will, jumping from world to world. Do you feel like moving had any kind of impact on you that shows up in your fiction?

Hmm, most of the moving around was before I was particularly self-aware. My mom was eighteen when I was born and a single mom, and we rambled all over the south mostly (some Missouri and Texas too), but we settled in North Carolina when I was five or six, so it felt pretty stable. (A lot of my deep psychological wiring certainly comes from those formative years, but I don't remember much.) I always liked road trips, though, and love seeing new places. When I went to college, I moved about as far as I could while keeping in-state tuition, to the mountains of North Carolina, where they had this weird stuff called "snow." After college I loaded up and drove across the country to California to see what was up out here. I honestly expected to be more itinerant than I am, but I met my wife, had a kid, got a job I liked at *Locus* instead of the succession of crap-jobs-while-writing-on-the-side I'd envisioned, and put down roots. (When my kid graduates high school, I may do some more rambling, but he's only a teen so it'll be a while.)

Doors of Sleep is written as a series of journal entries relaying the story of Zax's travels. Did you experiment with perspective and land on this style as the best for the story, or was the book conceived with this style in mind?

I started writing about Zax a few years ago in stories for my Patreon, and though the character changed a lot between the stories and the novel, they were always first person. The literal journal aspect came later, and I chose it for the book because it allowed me to play with point of view (my favorite thing!) by having other people take up the story and write in Zax's journal occasionally. I was also inspired by various other travelogues, written in the first person; I love Bill Bryson's various accounts of his journeys, and Jerome K. Jerome's fiction/memoir hybrid *Three Men in a Boat* is a longtime favorite.

What are the advantages and the challenges of this approach, and how did you deal with the challenges?

With a diary format you're not even inside a character's head; you're reading the things that character chooses to write down, which is a challenge and an advantage. Unreliable narration is always a treat; Zax tries to be pretty honest, but like anyone, he emphasizes some things and elides others. The big limitation is that you're stuck with just a single point of view, but of course, I cheated and had other people write stuff down in his journal for various reasons a couple of times in the novel. It's a format that's great for building suspense, because the character can say, "This is what we're going to do," and any experienced reader of fiction will *know* it won't work out that way.

While Doors of Sleep has this fantastical/wonder element to it, with a dazzle of tons of efficiently sketched worlds, there are also horror elements, and the suspense of the chase. The Zax and companion dynamic reminds me of Doctor Who, but through a journey that adds a dash of Rick and Morty. What is the heart of the story for you, what do you want people to know about this book?

My agent read the synopsis and said, "It's like *Doctor Who* combined with *Quantum Leap*," which is a good comp, if alas a bit dated. (I did like *Quantum Leap* when I was a kid.)

For me, the heart of things is Zax and his desire for connection, when he has a condition that makes lasting connection almost impossible. There's a reason I started the story with him finding Minna as a companion, instead of writing about one of the other companions he lost or who chose to leave him; she wants to stick by him, and sees him as more than a ticket to a better life. Minna values Zax on his own merits, and he was so desperate for that. And later they're joined by Vicki, who just hungers for knowledge and new information, and traveling with Zax is a perfect way to get a never-ending stream of new data. Zax gets to be not so alone, for a while at least, but there's always the constant danger of being separated from them forever, which is a nice drumbeat of suspense.

Sometimes new writers will ask "how do you know who your main character should be," and one traditional answer is, "whoever would suffer the most," and that's Zax: trained as a harmonizer, a sort of social worker, he does his best to help people and make meaningful connections, but he always has to leave, so he never knows if he made a lasting difference. He's a character who is lucky to ever get beyond the lowest tier on the hierarchy of needs, and even attaining *that* tier is a frequent challenge.

Felix, the protagonist in The Fractured Void, starts out in a very different situation: he's been rewarded with command of a ship, but punished by being shoved off to a region of space that is ostensibly boring. How would you compare Felix and Zax—and in what ways do you relate to them most?

They're pretty different! Felix's big flaw is that he acts too impulsively and doesn't think consequences through as much as he should. I punish him in this novel by giving him what he wants: excitement, real responsibility, a challenging mission . . . and it's mostly awful and painful and dangerous. He's also pathologically self-confident and happy to solve problems with violence, whereas Zax does his very best to eschew violent solutions. What they have in common is a deep affection for their friends and the understanding that you do better as a team than you do going it alone.

Will readers who loved the Axiom books find The Fractured Void just as tasty? Are there important similarities that will delight fans; or is it really speaking to a different audience?

I got the gig writing *The Fractured Void* because of the Axiom books, so probably! It's a tie-in to the legendary Twilight Imperium strategy board game, a brain-meltingly complex space opera world with lots of alien species and cultures and multiple overlapping axes of conflict. Editor Marc Gascoigne is the one who bought the first Axiom novel when he was at Angry Robot, and when he moved over to Aconyte and took on the Twilight Imperium project, he thought of me. (He says "when he jotted down T IMP my handwriting rendered it as TIM P so it was obviously a sign from the heavens.") There's certainly the same sense of found family I have in the Axiom books, and banter, and snark. The antagonists in *The Fractured Void* are more sympathetic than the Axiom or their allies (who are just super awful, because writing villains like that is fun sometimes). In fact, my favorite characters in the book are the duo who pursue Felix: Severyne and Azad, operatives from rival polities forced to work together against a common enemy, who develop a really great frenemy vibe.

Are the Axiom books really over, or do you have more fiction planned for that universe?

I wanted to wrap up the main story in a trilogy, but I didn't tell all the stories I had in that world. I did a Kickstarter for a collection called *The Alien Stars*, and that's coming out in the near future: It's three novellas, each about a character from the original trilogy who didn't get sufficient time to shine, in my opinion: the cyborg engineer Ashok, the alien Lantern, and the artificial intelligence Shall. The novellas turned out *really well.* I'm super happy with them and was so glad to return to that world.

We see a number of creatives utilizing Patreon and similar platforms to generate income and perhaps even to make the most of their creative property. Is Patreon a good model for most authors, is it the future of publishing? Or is it a platform some will find hard to utilize to significant effect?

The mantra of all freelancers should be "multiple revenue streams." Patreon is one of my many streams. Some people make a living from Patreon, but I couldn't; I guess I'm a Patreon mid-lister, pulling in $700 or so a month (sometimes more, sometimes less, but I've been doing it for five and a half years and it's pretty stable now). That's not at *all* bad for a short story, especially since I sell some of them as reprints later. I started the Patreon less for money than for art (though I like money); I love short fiction, but wasn't writing much because novels had taken over, and I knew if I promised people a story every month, I'd re-center short fiction in my creative life. That's been awesome. I don't think stuff like this is necessarily the future, but it's part of *a* future.

As for whether it's good for other authors . . . if you have a readership already, and want to commit to an ongoing thing, for sure. You can't crowdfund without a crowd. If no one is listening, it doesn't matter how beautifully you sing, you know? I had the advantage of a proven track record quality-wise as a short fiction writer, and I'd done a lot of crowdfunding in the past, so I also had an audience that trusted me to deliver what I promised. (I haven't missed a month yet! Though a couple of them were squeakers. I keep thinking I should write a bunch of extra stories to have in inventory in case of disaster, but I keep not doing that.)

My friend *Toby Buckell* says crowdfunding is a three-legged stool. I'm just gonna quote him. There's "a leg of having a strong social media presence and profile. A leg of haven proven that you can deliver on the project and have delivered in the past. And lastly, a leg of a project that is compelling in and of itself." Ideally you have all three. I did, though a couple of the legs were maybe shakier. If you do, yeah, go for it. If you have two of them and they're really strong, go for it then too. Otherwise, could be hard.

One of your recent Patreon stories, "Last Halloween," is a horror short featuring a young woman who revisits some of the most terrible moments of her life. What is the allure of horror for you, and what makes a great piece of horror fiction?

One of the things that interests me as a writer is exploring how characters react psychologically to extreme circumstances, and terror and dread elicit such reactions. I also just love monsters and creepy shit and nightmare logic and the sense of reality coming apart underneath you. That stuff appeals to me on a very basic level that resists any kind of explanation or analysis. The horror stories I love best are the ones where there's a sense of dread that gradually builds and then there's a *snap* at the end. (Ray Vukcevich's "Whisper" is one of my favorite horror stories, right up there with Kelly Link's "Monster.")

I also like horror that's rooted in the character's experience, past, or personality. Not necessarily in the sense that they brought it on themselves, just that their horror experience connects somehow psychologically to their personal circumstances. I do enjoy the school of horror where bad stuff comes out of nowhere and characters just have to deal—that's a lot of Stephen King's work, and he was the first horror writer I ever read—because that's life; you get natural disasters, you get cancer, you get run over, life turns on you. But even in those cases, I want the way the character reacts to be unusual in some way because that reaction is informed by their past and personality. Horror where a sort of generic every-person runs away from a monster doesn't work for me. The monster should never be more interesting than the person they're trying to eat.

What do you consider to be some of the best horror you ever wrote, and why?

I did one on my Patreon called "Through the Woods" that I like a lot, with a kind of classic premise: dysfunctional couple have a car break down in the woods on the way to Thanksgiving and bad stuff happens and hard choices have to be made. I had another called "Fool's Fire" in *PseudoPod* about the dark gods of the GPS, the successors to will-o'-the-wisps who use to lead people to their deaths in the woods; now they're the ones who trick people into driving off bridges or into lakes or down dead-end streets in bad parts of town. Probably the best one I've written in years was "Sometimes You Get the Bear," set in a world where, whenever a person is about to die of any cause at all, a giant spectral cave bear comes and kills them. Then a guy decides to go on a bear hunt to kill death. That's in my collection *Miracles & Marvels.*

Looking at your short fiction, which are the stories that stand out most for you, which are most important to you, and why?

"Little Gods" started my career in a lot of ways; it was a Nebula finalist (thanks, short fiction jury!) and was the title piece of my debut collection. "Hart and Boot" was in *The Best American Short Stories 2005* (thanks, Michael Chabon!), and *that* didn't hurt; it was the title piece in my second collection. "Impossible Dreams" won a Hugo (thanks, Hugo voters!). That's probably the holy triumvirate in terms of influence on my career, being reprinted a bunch, etc.

More personally, I love my story "Cup and Table" from *Twenty Epics* and reprinted at *PodCastle*, because it was challenging structurally, and I totally nailed the ending. "Another End of the Empire" at *Strange Horizons* is the only story I've written that came out on the page *exactly* the way I saw it in my head. "Happy Old Year" at *Drabblecast* is my homage to *Twilight Zone* stories, so I was super happy when Benjamin DeHart made it into short film *The New Year.*

What are some of your favorite pieces reserved for your Patreon folks, and what do you like about those pieces?

I put most of my *very* favorites in *Miracles & Marvels* last year. From this year, "Beneath a Black Moon" is a story about gardening and transcendence and I think it turned out really well; I read Susanna Clarke's awesome *Piranesi* and started thinking about occult practitioners and that story bubbled up. (It doesn't have much in common with *Piranesi* besides those occult concerns, but those are the best inspirations, when you can't even see a clear connection, I think.)

"Revenance" is really cool; it's your classic horror story about someone who gets killed in a hit-and-run and returns as a spirit to exact revenge on the driver, but my spirit has ethical and moral concerns about murdering the person who killed him. "The Bodies" is about a guy who finds a dead body . . . and then another dead body another day . . . and then *another* . . . until it's clear something supernatural is up; that came from a conversation with my friend (and author! Her debut story is coming from *PseudoPod* next year!), Sarah Day, about people we knew of who'd discovered dead people (or in one case, a head) and how it messed them up.

Huh. Those are all horror stories. Why am I so focused on horror stories in this pandemic election year. Who can say.

What else are you working on, what else do you have coming up that you'd like readers to know about?

quiet sobbing I have a lot of deadlines. When I get anxious, I take on extra work, because it gives me a sense of control; you'd think knowing this about myself psychologically would allow me to do something about it, but no. A while back I decided to write four books by Fall 2021. One of them is done (*The Alien Stars*), one is in process (the second Twilight Imperium novel, *The Necropolis Empire*), and the other two will happen: a sequel to *The Doors of Sleep* and a project that cannot yet be confirmed but nevertheless looms before me. (It's fine, actually, I sat down with a calendar and worked it all out, there's enough time. The key is to not have any hobbies.) Oh, and my wife Heather Shaw and I are doing our traditional winter holiday collaborative story for *PodCastle* again this year! Those are always fun.

ABOUT THE AUTHOR

Arley Sorg is co-Editor-in-Chief at *Fantasy Magazine*. A 2014 Odyssey Writing Workshop graduate, he writes SF/F/H, reviews for *Cascadia Subduction Zone Magazine,* and is also associate editor at both *Locus* and *Lightspeed* magazines.

Editor's Desk: Don't Let Go of the Future

NEIL CLARKE

It's tempting to write a year-in-review editorial, but honestly, I don't feel up to writing about life-threatening surgery, pandemics, deaths, or the host of other stressful elements that make up this past year's highlights. It's pervasive and exhausting. We've all been through enough and I understand now why previous pandemics have been more-or-less removed from our cultural memory.

The big thing is that we're still here. You're still reading. Authors are still writing and submitting stories. Our team is still working. It's been a lot, but we've survived what's been thrown at us and maybe learned a few things in the process. I know I have.

In last month's editorial, I started talking about the future again for the first time in a while. In my previous careers, I noticed my discomfort with a job peaked if it shifted to maintenance mode, the state of just keeping things running. In trying to minimize stress, I thought a temporary maintenance mode would help. It didn't. Trying new things is a source of joy for me and I need to be working towards them now more than ever.

The Spanish-language project I spoke of is just one element of many. The reaction that announcement received was primarily positive and energetic. Sure, there are a few people who see anything that widens the arms of the submissions pool as a threat, but I've never rejected a story because I don't have room in inventory and that won't be starting now. Keep in mind that the pool already includes work from a wide variety of authors from around the world.

It also occurs to me that it is important to focus on increasing subscriptions and re-evaluating our pricing scheme right now. Authors, artists, and staff deserve to be paid real rates and I haven't been doing them (or myself) any favors by taking any changes off the table this year. I've seen a steady increase in new writers or artists submitting work (and others looking for jobs here) that state in their cover letters that they've been let go from their day jobs. If we can change our pay scales even a little, it's meaningful.

I've also been working on a ground-up redesign of the website. Something a bit more modern and flexible for where the new road leads us. I have to say that getting back into programming, even at the web scripting level, has been a pleasant distraction lately. Some of our Patreon and ClarkesworldCitizen supporters have seen early previews of the new design and offered a few suggestions. I'm hoping to share a bit more in public in the near future. If there's ever anything you wish we had on our website, this would be a good time to speak up.

It's good to be back to this part of the job and that is a great way to end a no good, very bad year.

ABOUT THE AUTHOR

Neil Clarke is the editor of *Clarkesworld Magazine* and *Forever Magazine;* owner of Wyrm Publishing; and a eight-time Hugo Award Nominee for Best Editor (short form). His anthologies include *Upgraded, Galactic Empires, More Human Than Human, Touchable Unreality, The Final Frontier, Not One of Us, The Eagle has Landed,* and the Best Science Fiction of the Years series. His most recent anthology, *The Best Science Fiction of the Year: Volume 5,* was published in October by Night Shade Books. He currently lives in NJ with his wife and two sons.

I Hear Them

COVER ART BY CLAUDIO PILIA

Claudio Pilia is a matte painter and concept artist. He finished his formal art education in 2014 in Berlin, where he enhanced his knowledge of drawing and painting techniques. His digital art skills are completely self-taught and he employs a combination of both traditional and digital methods in his work. While employed by Pixomondo, he put these skills to use on projects like *The Wandering Earth, Game of Thrones,* and *The Walking Dead.* Currently, he is a full time freelance concept artist helping to visualize ideas and create worlds.